The Stolen Bounty

Joe Shay was an Indian agent who had been notably successful in maintaining peace with the Indians, and all sides trusted him. But, one day in the peaceful frontier town of Massacre, it looked as if all that would end.

Into town rode a man reeling and caked in black, congealed blood. He had been scalped and immediately the hotheads wanted to take up arms against the local Cheyenne tribe.

It took all Joe's power of persuasion, not to mention the power of his fists, to convince the angry townsfolk to let him bring the murderers to justice. Now it was all down to him, his gun and his knife. One way or another he would surely earn his nickname – Cheyenne Joe.

The Stolen Bounty

A Black Horse Western

ROBERT HALE · LONDON

ISBN 0 7090 7311 9

Robert Hale Limited
Clerkenwell House
Clerkenwell Green
London EC1R 0HT

Typeset by
Derek Doyle & Associates, Liverpool.
Printed and bound in Great Britain by
Antony Rowe Limited, Wiltshire

CHAPTER ONE

INDIAN TROUBLE!

All in one second, Massacre blew up. One moment the dreary little frontier town on the edge of the rushing Smoky Hill River was at peace with itself – as near to peace, that is, as ever it could be. The next it seemed to erupt with fury and passion at sight of that lone rider who had come flogging his horse down the dusty main street.

Night was fast approaching when he was first seen, so that he came into town silhouetted against the final glow of the sun that was dying beyond the Sawatch Mountains; there were lights coming on in the saloons and gaming establishments, and the board walks were beginning to throng with men seeking relaxation after a day of torrid Colorado heat.

They turned, as men usually turn when they hear the approach of a hard-driven horse. They saw him – reeling and caked with black, congealed blood. He was a nightmare figure on top of that half-dead little mustang.

He halted outside the Kansas–Colorado Overland Freight Corporation's office, alongside the saloon called Red Eye. For a moment he just sat and swayed, his half-closed eyes glazed and distant with utter exhaustion. Men

5

came running towards him, and he seemed at last to see them, to realize that he had attained his objective.

They heard his voice and it was cracked and uncertain because of the strain that he had passed through; he sounded maudlin, even more than a bit drunk, but they knew he wasn't drunk, wasn't rambling. They knew it because of what they could see.

The lone rider quavered. 'Injuns did it. They've bust out – ridin' the war trails agen. They attacked Luther's Crossin' – killed Mark Luther an' his wife. Rode down the valley an' scalped every white man, woman an' child—'

He was sagging in his saddle now, his strength ebbing suddenly away. And as he drooped lower, so his voice went quieter until it could hardly be heard, and now there was a moan with his words.

'Sandy Crawford an' his wife – I saw 'em took an' killed. An' Lem Holley an' Mike Cousen an' Rupe Elliot an' – an' others.' He was nearly out of his saddle now, but he found strength for a few more words. 'They got me, tortured me, but I got away—'

Then he toppled headlong out of the saddle, before anyone had the presence of mind to catch him. He crumpled into the dust close by the broken board walk, and the yellow light from the saloon called Red Eye fell on him as he lay motionless there.

And it was at that moment that the town of Massacre seemed to blow up.

For men saw now what they could not see before, when that rider was up there in his saddle. They saw a man who had been scalped alive.

He was dead when they bent over him. He had lived long enough to get warning through to them that the Indians were on the warpath again, and then he had died.

There was a roar of ferocious, fever-hot rage. Men shouted with savage hate because of the barbarous treatment of their fellow white man. And at the noise more and more people came running up until the street was packed solid from the livery stable right down to the saddler's.

For a few minutes blind fury took their senses from them, and they swayed, packed together, and raved against the murdering red man, and the noise was terrifying to hear. And then men of action began to be heard – but they were men of primitive reaction, and what they demanded was – revenge!

They called for men to take to arms and ride against the marauders, and within seconds the cry had been taken up and went swelling into a mighty roar, and men began to hurry away to saddle up and get arms and provisions for a campaign in the Mark Luther country.

Back among the crowd a man had stood listening. He was much like the other men, simply, roughly dressed. Perhaps a little taller than most, perhaps straighter, like a man who has seen military service. A lean, hardy-looking frontiersman, browned by many summers and winters of exposure to fierce sun and icy winds. He wore the fringed buckskin trousers and jacket that were conventional in the far West of that day, and a battered, broad-rimmed hat that was bleached colourless by years of exposure. He began to move when the crowd lifted its hoarse voice in a demand for retribution, began to push his way through the throng towards the loading stage of the freight company. He was a determined man, and bundled his way through to the front without heed to the curse words that greeted his forcefulness.

The inevitable mob orator had risen to harangue the crowd. He was a lumbering, coarse-faced, hoarse-voiced teamster with vicious eyes: the kind of man who thrives on trouble, who revels in destruction, and connives always at disorder. A trouble-maker!

That determined man who had stood among the crowd vaulted on to the loading stage beside the shouting man. Almost contemptuously, it seemed, he pitched the fellow headlong into the crowd; then he stood there looking out at the irate mob, his face expressionless, his hands loose at his sides.

A shout of anger had gone up at sight of their orator

7

being so summarily removed, but even as it was issuing from the mouths of those men there, it was checked and a curious silence fell on the crowd – a silence broken only by a few muttered words – 'Cheyenne Joe! That's Cheyenne Joe hisself!'

He looked down on them, Cheyenne Joe, with eyes that were calm and completely unafraid. He was a man very sure of himself, a man who had faced death on countless occasions and had kept on living because of his very boldness.

He was a legend in the West, Joe Shay. No one knew of his early origins; he had come up with the frontier as pioneers pressed deeper and deeper into the American continent. For a time he had ridden as a scout for the army and had hunted for buffalo for the commissariat.

Then he had become entrusted as a carrier of peace terms to the warring Indian tribes, and it was then that his name had become a legend.

He had gone where men said no white man could go and remain alive. For weeks he had ridden inside Indian territory, seeking out the Indian villages and riding boldly in on them, then sitting down patiently to talk peace to men who wanted war.

When he came back it was to say that peace could be negotiated; that the Teton Dakota, the Crow, Blackfoot, Cheyenne and Arapaho people would bury the hatchet if reasonable terms were offered them. The President himself had eagerly offered terms, and the bold white hunter had gone back and talked the Indians into accepting them.

When that was done, and the Indians had moved to their appointed reservations, he had gone to act as Indian agent to the Cheyenne tribe within their territory – and Joe Shay became Cheyenne Joe from that date.

When there was quiet, the Indian agent spoke. He had a deep voice, a voice that seemed to growl – the voice of a man who used it sparingly, and when he did it carried emphasis even to the point of aggression.

He looked at the mob, their rough faces illuminated by the saloon lights, and he told them: 'You c'n forget about takin' arms agen the Injuns in Luther country. This ain't no uprisin'; it's the work of some bad Injuns – maybe two or three dozen, but not a band or a tribe.'

Someone shouted, 'How d'you know?'

Cheyenne Joe looked over the heads in the direction of the speaker, and answered tersely, 'I was with the Cheyenne a couple of days ago. They weren't talkin' war then, an' I know 'em well enough to know they wouldn't change their minds in forty-eight hours.'

'How about Arapaho?' That was another shout.

The Indian agent shook his head. 'Why should Arapaho come eighty miles just to kill in Luther country when there's plenty whites within a few miles of 'em?' It was sufficient answer.

He spoke so assuredly, was so certain in his knowledge of the red man, that it stilled the querulous tongues of the ones eager for war.

He went on, 'Leave this to me. If these Injuns are Cheyenne, the chiefs will hand them over when I ask. They've always done it, an' I reckon they'll do it this time, too. An' the military will take care of them, you c'n bet.'

The crowd hesitated, torn between respect for this celebrated scout and hunter and a natural desire to exact revenge on the miscreants. Then one man stood right before them and challenged Cheyenne Joe.

'The hell,' he shouted, 'what're you listenin' to this fellar for? Let's settle with them blamed Injuns ourselves!'

It was the coarse-faced, hoarse-voiced teamster, inflamed with fury at the way he had been so easily ejected from the loading platform. Cheyenne Joe looked down into small, brown, raging eyes and went on the alert immediately. This was the killer look if he had ever seen it.

And Joe could feel the quick sympathy that came from the crowd at those words. This crowd was thirsting for blood; right with them was the corpse of a man who had been treated abominably, and they wanted to hear nothing but talk of revenge.

They began to shout, began to press forward, so that a great surging mass seethed right up against the loading platform.

'We c'n do the job as good as the army!'

'The varmints'll have got away by the time they get troops up the Smoky!'

'You keep your nose out of this, Cheyenne, an' leave it to us!'

The hunter heard, and was quick to realize that if they weren't stopped they would inflame each other into madness by their own wild talk.

He stopped them by raising his hands and shouting until they quietened to listen to him.

'You fools,' he told them bluntly. 'Do you know what would happen if you followed this critter's advice?' He looked round, awaiting an answer, but nothing came from the men but a low sullen murmur. 'You'd ride out an' you'd fall on the first Injun village you came to an' you'd kill every Injun you could lay your hands on. You wouldn't ask if they were the guilty people—'

'Hell, ain't one Injun as bad as another?' someone shouted.

'Nope,' returned Cheyenne Joe decisively. 'There's good Injuns an' bad Injuns – just the same as there's good whites an' a lot of no-good trash. And it's the trash that wants you to go out killin' innocent Injuns, an' if you did that you'd set the land alight agen – you'd bring all the Injuns out of the reservations an' we'd have war!'

He shouted into the gathering darkness, 'You men who have wives an' children, you don't want war agen, do you?' There was a quick growl at that, and when he heard it. Joe knew he was winning. He was talking sense into some of the men at least.

'All right, then, leave it to me an' to the military to deal with this situation. Go back to your homes an' keep your hands near your guns.' Then he added, surely and with confidence, 'Though I'll take a bet them Injuns isn't within miles of Luther country now and won't do no more harm!'

It was that absolute assurance of the man that swayed them. He was so completely certain; he so palpably knew his Indians and their ways, that no one, no matter how hot their blood ran right at that moment, felt inclined to oppose him publicly.

There were so many who wanted to, and they muttered meanly to each other under their breath and shuffled their feet awkwardly, but they hadn't the courage to stand up to him.

So when he was assured that he had quietened the mob Cheyenne Joe dropped from the platform and pushed his way out through the crowd. He was joined by a man who looked as round as a cart wheel – a small, grey-haired man with humorous little eyes that peeped out from folds of fat. He was the proprietor the Red Eye saloon, and a good friend of the Indian agent's. He was one of the few saloon keepers who resolutely kept the law and refused to sell firewater to the Indians, and for that Cheyenne Joe liked him.

Rotund little Andy Coan said, 'Reckon a passel of angry white men don't trouble you none at all, Joe.'

Cheyenne Joe retorted, 'I get paid to do a job, Andy, so I do it. My job's to stop trouble between Injuns an' whites. You know how things are – it wouldn't take much to start another Injun war, an' you know how much the last one cost.'

Andy Coan said, bitterly, 'Nine hundred lives lost in the fighting agen the Cheyenne alone, an' a three million dollar bill for the taxpayer to foot.' He spat unpleasantly. 'An' me, I'm the biggest taxpayer around these parts, I reckon.'

Cheyenne Joe prodded him good-humouredly in his most prominent feature and was saying, 'You sure are the biggest, Andy,' when he heard a word spoken against him.

The crowd had started to disperse, turning their weathered features towards the attractive brightnesses of the saloons and gaming parlours, when one man shouted, 'Renegade!'

Cheyenne Joe wheeled. The crowd had parted to show the teamster standing there, his heavy face lowering with anger and evil passion. He had been humbled before this crowd, and now, suddenly, recklessly, he wanted to settle scores with the man who had done it. In that moment he forgot about the reputation of the hunter – forgot caution, everything. He was as near to being a madman as ever anger can turn a brain.

The Indian agent marched steadily back to where the slanderer stood and swayed. Cheyenne Joe thought, 'Guess this fellar's got some liquor in him.' It made the man the more dangerous. He was a stranger around the town, probably a team driver for the big immigrant train that was camped west along the flats.

Cheyenne Joe rapped, 'Was that word intended for me?'

They faced each other, glaring – a big, lumpish creature, gross and brutal, and a finely built, strong, intelligent young frontiersman.

The teamster snarled, 'Who else? I've heard of you, Cheyenne Joe. The Injun agent – the man who works for the Injuns!'

The crowd pressed round the men, forming a close, eager, breathless circle. Cheyenne Joe could feel their warm breath on his neck, saw the yellow light reflecting on perspiring faces. He didn't like being hemmed in so closely and flung out his arms to press back the spectators.

While he was standing there, arms extended, the teamster jumped in and hit him. The first blows landed before Cheyenne Joe could put up his hands to guard himself, and they were hard blows that rocked him by their very weight. He felt blood run down from a cut eye, and there was the taste of hot, salty blood in his mouth as he drew back from the stinging blows.

Then he walked into that teamster and gave him the thrashing of his life. It was something the heavy man had never expected, not from a lighter built fellow like Cheyenne Joe. The teamster had reckoned that in a close fight, with a pressing crowd to restrict movement, he would be able to use his greater weight and apparent strength and crush his opponent by sheer force.

But it didn't work like that. The teamster saw the big young hunter rock back as his bunched, hairy fists smashed into that brown face. He gloated in triumph to feel his blows landing home, and he lurched forward again with the intention of pounding his opponent to jelly,

But his opponent apparently didn't intend to become jelly – not at the teamster's hands. The teamster saw a fist travelling towards him. It crashed flat on his nose. It was the most tremendous blow that the teamster had ever received in a lifetime filled with savage blows.

He gasped and then moaned with the shock of the pain. There was blood cascading down his coarse, brutal face, and he knew in that instant that the one blow from Cheyenne Joe had broken his nose.

He didn't have time to recover. The Indian agent was in a hurry to leave Massacre, and he jumped in to finish his opponent in quick time.

The crowd started to roar its approval. All crowds are against the fellow who strikes a first, treacherous blow, and if the opponent survives it and then comes back, they love it.

Cheyenne Joe could hear a tremendous bellow which started only a couple of yards away from him. It began to go higher and higher as he pitched into the staggering teamster.

The crowd had wanted action, and this fight was like a safety valve that released their passions. They saw the younger, lither man just walk right into his opponent, his fists stabbing, hooking and cutting into that big head, sending it jolting back on to the thick bull-neck as if at any moment it would be knocked off.

They had never expected it. Cheyenne Joe finished his adversary in less than a minute. At the end of that time the teamster was a dazed and battered hulk on the ground.

When Cheyenne Joe knew that his opponent had no more fight left in him, he stood over him and let his hard grey eyes travel round the circle of spectators. They quietened, to hear what he had to say.

He said softly: 'Any other man that thinks I'm a renegade had better keep his tongue quiet or this'll happen to him, too.' Challengingly he looked again round the ring. He was ready to take on all-comers at that moment, but no one stepped forward to take him up. 'I'm no renegade!' he snapped angrily. 'I work for the white man's interest perhaps even more than the red man's.'

Abruptly he turned and shoved his way through the throng. Andy Coan saw his face as he forced his way across the front of the Red Eye Saloon, and he realized that the Indian agent was hurt. He was a sensitive man, this Cheyenne Joe, and it was bitterness to him that because he lived with the Indians and acted as their representative he should be regarded as a renegade of his own kind.

Andy Coan thought shrewdly: 'This ain't the first time he's had that word thrown at him. Reckon he's gettin' a bit tired of bein' called renegade.'

Which was about it. Cheyenne Joe, going across to his horse, thought 'Whenever a fellar gets so's he don't like me he starts to call me names – but they're always the same.'

Renegade – traitor – white Injun. He was getting very tired of it. Well, he thought, with a return of his normal good humour, one fellar would be careful of his words in future.

He was mounting, swinging into his creaking saddle, when he heard his name called. It came from the darkness, from the shadow round the corner of the Red Eye.

'Hey, thar, Cheyenne!'

Cheyenne stooped in the saddle and peered against the light. He made out a tall, lean figure wearing a cap with coonskin tails. That and the voice established the stranger to be a Kentuckian.

Cheyenne was suspicious. His hand slipped to the Colt on his belt. It wasn't healthy to speak to men who stood back in the shadows.

'What do you want?' he demanded, and he was careful not to admit that he was Cheyenne Joe. He didn't want a bullet in his face.

'I want ter talk to you,' came the soft voice.

Cheyenne Joe shook his head. 'I've done enough talkin' fer one night.' He pulled his horse's head round so that it faced west along the main street. 'I've got to get back to my Injuns.'

He must make all haste to see the Cheyenne chiefs and find out if Cheyennes were responsible for the outbreak in Luther country. He thought, 'If they are, the Cheyennes'll hand 'em over to the military.' The Cheyennes had kept scrupulously to their word, and had themselves punished any violators of the peace terms within their midst. He was confident they would do it again.

The Kentuckian stepped forward at that, so that Cheyenne saw that he carried an old-fashioned long gun – that five-foot long gun that had made history in the West. Even so, Cheyenne noticed that he still hugged the shelter of the Red Eye Saloon, as if he didn't want to be seen talking to the Indian agent. He had a beard that stuck out like a goat's, and a dress that was buckskin throughout. He looked a real old-timer, thought Cheyenne, and was somewhat reassured by the sight.

That old Kentucky voice said: 'Thar's friends come in with the immigrant train today, Cheyenne – the men you're lookin' for.'

Cheyenne exclaimed in surprise: 'How do you know I'm lookin' for anyone?'

'I heard your name mentioned. They said they was to meet up with you in Massacre.'

15

The Indian agent nodded. That was right; that was how it had been arranged. He was to meet the Washington representatives in Massacre when he arrived.

'Are you with the party?' he asked.

The Kentuckian shook his head. 'Nope. I'm with the immigrant train, an' the Indian Office commissioner an' his bodyguard is travellin' with us fer company.'

Cheyenne's heart leapt. A bodyguard – that meant they had brought the bounty! And if the bounty came through it would stop the muttering and discontent among the tribesmen in consequence of a hard winter and late spring on the reservation.

Cheyenne began to dismount at that, and then he paused, half out of the saddle, his old suspicions returned. 'Why don't you come out into the open, stranger, 'stead of holdin' to them shadows like you do? You afraid of something?'

'Nope.' It was a decisive enough answer. 'But I reckon thar's folks might think things ef they see me talkin' to you, Cheyenne.'

Something in the way the man spoke dispelled completely the Indian agent's suspicions. He came down off his horse and walked into the shadows to where the Kentuckian was standing.

'I don't know what's on your mind, stranger, but I'll hear you. You got something to tell me?'

The Kentuckian answered reluctantly. 'Waal, not exactly. I reckon I'm just a naturally suspicious man, an' I've heard things I shouldn't. Maybe I'm gettin' 'em wrong; maybe I ain't.'

He'd been riding guard around the immigrant camp one night, and he was passing the tent of Captain Galbray when he heard a snatch of conversation.

'Cap'n Galbray's got a dozen cavalry with him to guard that wagon they're takin' through. I could see him an' another fellar – just shadows in the lamplight agen the tent. I heard the fellar say, "It's a downright shame to give Injuns all them dollars".'

The Kentuckian paused, and Cheyenne said impatiently: 'Go on, old-timer. What did the captain say to that?'

'That's just it, Cheyenne. The captain didn't say anythin'. He just sat there, not movin' an inch. An' the fellar said again, "It's a shame, cap'n, just as I said. A downright shame". I think he said it again after that, too, but I couldn't hear too well because he spoke very softly.'

'And then what happened?'

'The cap'n didn't speak, an' the other fellar came out of the tent.'

He paused, and the pause was so significant that Cheyenne knew the Kentuckian wanted him to ask: 'Who was the fellar?' So he asked the question.

'It was Wade Pengelly, the commissioner hisself.'

'I see,' said Cheyenne.

The old-timer went on: 'I don't reckon much to any of them agents back from Washington. Most of 'em are just plain thieves – just a bunch of scallawags an' carpetbaggers. They work for the Government, but they rob it all they can.'

Cheyenne nodded. He, too, had little respect for the rogues who came west on Government service. He was an Indian agent himself, working for the Indian Office, but he knew that around the department in Washington had collected all the scum and rogues in the East. They robbed the taxpayer and cheated the red man they were supposed to help.

'Looks like that commissioner fellar plans to help hisself to the bounty money he's supposed to bring through to me,' he said softly. 'That your idea, too, old-timer?'

The honest old Kentuckian said: 'I cain't figure it no other way.'

'But the cap'n wasn't bein' talked into helpin'?'

'He wasn't agreein', but he wasn't sayin' no, either.'

'No.' Cheyenne sighed softly. 'An' when a fellar doesn't say no to a hundred thousand United States dollars I

17

reckon he's maybe figgerin' on sayin' yes ultimately.'

'Don't know what that word means,' the cautious old Kentuckian answered. 'But ef you mean he'll be sayin' yes by tomorrow, I sure wouldn't disagree with you.' He spat. 'Trouble is, I was seen by the commissioner, sittin' out there on my hoss. He looked a bit startled, so I guess he knew I'd heard more'n was good for him.'

'That's why you don't want to be seen talkin' to me?'

'Thar's plenty of men in town tonight who came in with that train. That fellar you licked just now, he's teamster fer the commissioner's prairie wagon.'

'So we might meet again.' The thought didn't worry the hunter. He'd licked the teamster once, and he reckoned he could do it again if the fellow got awkward.

He stirred. 'I must be on my way, old-timer. I want to get them Injuns that started the rumpus in Luther country, but I'll call in on the commissioner on my way out.' He thought: 'The commissioner was goin' to be here in Massacre this evenin'. Why hasn't he turned up?' He felt disturbed at the thought that the commissioner might be playing a deep game with him.

He mounted. The Kentuckian still kept to the shadows. Cheyenne spoke softly. 'I sure am grateful to you, pard. Thank God there's a few honest men left in the West!'

The Kentuckian said gruffly: 'You don't need to thank me, mister. I only did what I know was right to do.' He spat. 'It's the way you're brung up, I reckon.'

Cheyenne agreed. 'It's the way you're brung up, pard. So long!' And he rode out into the blackness of a moonless prairie.

When he'd gone, two shadows went across and stood by the Kentuckian. One of them said: 'You was talkin' to that Injun agent, wasn't you?'

And then the second one said: 'What was you tellin' him?' and his voice was low with menace.

The Kentuckian knew he was going to die, but his voice was very calm. 'I told him all I knew,' he said, and then the gun in his ribs went off and the old man slid down against the split-board wall of the saloon called Red Eye.

He was dying, but his final words held a note of philosophy: 'It's as I said. It's the way ... you're ... brung up ...'

And he was dead, alone there in the shadows, when they found him seconds later.

CHAPTER TWO

VENGEANCE!

The immigrant camp was less than a mile out of the town, rather north of the trail that led to the Cheyenne country. He guessed that the immigrants would be heading for the new strikes in California and would be aiming to reach the Colorado River which provided a pass through the mountain range. This would be the place of parting with the commissioner, who would be heading for the Cheyenne country around the foot of Pikes Peak.

He saw the lights of the camp when he came over a rise, and he picked his way cautiously over the rough ground until he came up to it.

There were many fires, and most of the big prairie schooners had lamps lit inside them. So near to Massacre, that town that had got its name from the Indian devastation of some years before, the new settlers had little need for caution.

All the same, Cheyenne thought they were too careless, for he rode through the circle of wagons without being challenged. It was different, though, when he approached the solitary covered wagon parked right in the centre of the circle.

Two soldiers were on guard, one at either end of the prairie schooner, and they were very much on the alert. When Cheyenne came riding up he was immediately challenged and made to dismount before he could approach. Evidently the captain of the guard was taking no chances on a robbery occurring while he was in charge of the money. Not, thought Cheyenne ironically, unless he had a share in the loot, maybe.

There was a tent pitched close to the wagon, and a light was shining inside, showing up the occupants as shadows against the yellow cloth. There were two men sitting at a table inside. Cheyenne thought: 'That's how it must have looked to the old Kentuckian that night.'

At the sentry's challenge the shadows moved and one came outside. 'Who's that, trooper?' queried a voice sharply.

Cheyenne answered for the man. 'My name's Shay – Joe Shay. I'm Injun agent in Cheyenne territory.'

The man seemed to hesitate. Because he had his back to the lamp he was just a silhouette to Cheyenne Joe, yet even so the agent felt that he was a little disturbed at the mention of his name.

Even so it was momentary, and afterwards Cheyenne thought that he might have been mistaken. The man turned and Cheyenne caught the gleam of light reflecting on buttons and guessed this would be Captain Jules Galbray of the 7th US Cavalry.

Galbray called: 'Come right this way, Shay! I guess you're welcome.' It was a brusque, unmusical, military voice, though the owner tried to infuse some cordiality into it. He was not noticeably successful.

Galbray ducked back into the tent, and Cheyenne followed. Some boxes and a crude table formed the furnishings of the low tent. A man stood ready to greet the Indian agent, his head bent forward in order to avoid touching the sloping eave.

He was a rather big man, rather heavy, especially around the thighs and lower limbs. His face was intelligent-looking, healthily pink, and altogether he was a handsome, impressive man.

Cheyenne said: 'Glad to meet you, commissioner.' He

21

paused and shot a quick glance at the man. 'I was expectin' to meet you in town this evenin'. Your message said before sunset.'

'I'm sorry.' Commissioner Pengelly spread his hands in apology. 'We pulled in later than we expected, so I thought maybe tomorrow mornin' would do just as well.'

Cheyenne wondered if that was an excuse; if, in fact, the commissioner, for some reason, had planned to slip through into Cheyenne territory without his company. It didn't make sense, but all the same the thought came to the agent.

'You got the bounty?'

Pengelly nodded. Cheyenne went on:

'It's a month overdue. The Injuns were gettin' restive. Food's not over-plentiful on the reservation, an' there's less fur tradin' to help 'em get by. That reservation ain't big enough for a few thousand Injuns.'

Pengelly rose. 'Yeah, the money's here. Good Yankee dollars.' The way he said it made Cheyenne sure the man was from the Deep South. He also had an idea that for all his smooth talk and Eastern rig-out he was a man who knew the West.

The commissioner ducked out of the tent. Cheyenne stood aside to let the captain go after him, and got his first real glimpse of the man's face.

Captain Galbray was a typical army officer. He led a hard life, and he looked a hard man. At first sight he looked thin, but Cheyenne knew it was the leanness that comes with a lifetime spent in the saddle; his face was gaunt, and the sun had browned his high cheekbones in a way that gave him an Indian appearance. But there was no Indian blood in him, Cheyenne was sure.

As they walked across to the wagon they heard a woman crying distantly. Galbray asked one of the sentries 'What's she cryin' for?' His voice was callous.

The trooper shifted his wad, spat, and said: 'They found her old man shot up alongside the Red Eye.'

Galbray shrugged indifferently. 'They should keep

22

away from saloons, these old-timers. They get so they can't look after themselves.'

By this time Pengelly had climbed into the wagon and had lit an oil lamp. He spoke down to the agent. 'Here it is, Mr Shay. One hundred thousand good American dollars.' He laughed. 'Just think what you could do with a hundred thousand green birds.'

The moon was rising now, and they were able to see more men riding in towards the camp. They came through the circle and slowly approached the commissioner's wagon. Cheyenne saw the gleam of buttons and guessed they were troopers returning from an evening in town.

Pengelly leaned against the tailboard and made small talk. Cheyenne realized that the army captain was standing very close to him in the dark, too, and he had a sudden feeling that Galbray was waiting for something. He was just not quite at ease.

Cheyenne said slowly: 'This outbreak up in Luther country kind of upsets plans, commissioner. I'm goin' right back to find out who did the scalpin'.' He checked himself. Perhaps they hadn't heard yet about the murders at the Luther trading post.

'We heard about the trouble. A fellar rode in just ahead of you, Mr Shay, with the news. In fact, we were discussin' the matter when you came up.' He shrugged. 'We've got to pass through Luther country, haven't we? Wal, I guess we don't want to run into a lot of blood-crazy Injuns an' get robbed of the bounty.'

'As well as loose our scalps.' Captain Galbray spoke, almost for the first time in their conversation. 'What do you think of the situation, Shay?'

Cheyenne was watching the troopers unsaddle their mounts. He turned to the captain. 'I think the raid's at an end. We'll find it's the work of a few disgruntled braves who have gone back to their camp with their scalps an' booty. All the same, I agree that it might be askin' for trouble to move into Luther country right now. I reckon you'd better sit tight here for a few days until I get word to you that it's safe for you to enter the territory. Either that or I come an' lead you in myself.'

'You leavin' right now?' the commissioner asked.

'Sure. I don't want this to spread.' Cheyenne started to walk to his mount and the other men fell into step with him.

Pengelly said, 'You don't need to worry any about the bounty, Mr Shay. Captain Galbray's got a dozen first-class men as escort, and they'll keep thievin' hands off it till we give it over to the chiefs for distribution.'

'That's good to hear, commissioner,' said Cheyenne. He thought, 'That Kentuckian sure put some bad thoughts into my mind. This fellar's straight, I'll swear it.'

He mounted. 'That bounty's very important, I guess. The tribe's restless inside the reservation, an' if they thought Uncle Sam was cheatin' them, there's nothin' would hold 'em back.'

One of the troopers must have overheard his words. He was placing a blanket against his saddle alongside the wagon, preparatory to bedding down for the night. The way he did it, clumsily and with much fumbling, suggested that he had been drinking in the town.

The trooper spoke up. 'Give 'em some of their own medicine. That'll keep them Injuns back, I say.' He appeared to be more than a little drunk, and his speech was thick and slurred. 'I'd have gone with 'em, too, if I hadn't been a soldier.'

Galbray snapped, 'Hold your tongue, there. Speak when you're spoken to.'

But Cheyenne was coming off that horse very quickly, dismounting and striding over to the man. He pulled him up from his knees, so swiftly that the trooper hadn't time to protest.

The Indian agent demanded, 'What did you mean when you said you'd have gone with them? Gone with whom? Gone where?'

The trooper wrestled clumsily to pull those hands off

his tunic, and because he was standing now Cheyenne let him go.

'Hold up, there, I ain't done nothin' wrong!' He started to get maudlin, but the agent repeated his questions and the fellow got round to answering them in the end.

'Someone said they'd seen a band of redskins camped along Sycamore Creek. They were passin' through on their way to the big Cheyenne pow-wow, I reckon.'

'Well?' demanded the agent.

'Wal, some of the boys decided to go an' get revenge for what they'd done to the settlers in Luther counfry.'

'An' you'd have been one of 'em but for you duty as a soldier!' Cheyenne turned away abruptly, his heart inflamed with anger.

This was always how things happened. The hot-heads among the Indians went and scalped innocent white people, and then the hot-heads among the white went and committed even greater atrocities against some innocent redskins.

'Why in heck can't they go an' scalp each other!' Cheyenne swore under his breath, hurrying to his mount.

The others had heard the conversation and now Pengelly said, 'Sycamore Creek's a good way off the trail, Mr Shay.'

'All the same, I'll have to ride there first an' try to stop this slaughter,' Cheyenne told him grimly, swinging into the saddle again. For it would be slaughter. There'd be women and children with that band of Indians, and these ruffians wouldn't spare any of them, Cheyenne was sure.

'Good luck,' called Pengelly, and the captain nodded as if to wish him well, too. Cheyenne spurred towards the circle of wagons. As he approached, the woman's crying voice came louder, and without knowing why he steered his horse to where the weeping came from.

There was an old, grey-haired woman sitting up there on a pile of sacks within the covered wagon. Two silent men kept her company. They could have been her sons.

Cheyenne, out of respect, took off his hat as he rode

past the end of the wagon. When he was through he didn't gallop his horse immediately, but instead let it pick its way at a walk towards the trail.

For he was thinking – suddenly he had been given something to think about.

For a coonskin hat was clutched in the woman's worn old hands. The kind of hat that the old Kentuckian had worn back in Massacre.

He stirred after a while. He felt sure now that it was the old Kentuckian who had been shot back in town, and he wondered if the man had died because he had spoken of his suspicions to him, Indian Agent Joe Shay? If so, who had killed him?

Cheyenne's face became grim as those thoughts raced through his brain. Maybe Pengelly was a smoother man than he appeared. Maybe the commissioner ought to be watched . . .

He rode hard for the next hour, and fortunately the night sky was kind, and there was no cloud to deprive him of the bright half-moon overhead.

Before he came to Sycamore Creek, he knew he would be too late to avert trouble. All the way he had been hoping that he could catch up with the vengeful white men, but they seemed to have too good a lead on him.

He rode into Sycamore Creek, that pleasant, tree-lined gulch through which ran a tributary of Smoky Hill River. Ten minutes later he looked upon the scene of the massacre.

It must have been a small band of about fifteen people, for Cheyenne saw only three ruined tepees. Looking down at the devastation in the cold, silvery moonlight, Cheyenne could see how it had been done. The white men had come upon the sleeping camp and had poured bullets through the buffalo-hide lodges, killing or wounding most of the occupants while they slept. Then they had fallen on those who had struggled clear of their beds and hacked them to pieces with their knives and axes, so that everywhere in that little clearing there were still, mangled forms.

Some were women. And some were very small.

Cheyenne went walking round the camp to see if there was any who could be saved, but those Indians were very dead, even though their bodies still carried the warmth of life within them.

When he was satisfied that he could do nothing more in Sycamore Creek, he mounted and rode away. There was fury in his heart. Willingly at that moment he would have ridden against the ruffians who had perpetrated this awful deed and given up his own life in an attempt to punish them.

Joe Shay was no ordinary white man who believed that in all things the red man was at fault. He knew there were good and bad in both whites and reds – he knew it better than most palefaces because he lived with the red men and knew them intimately. And he didn't believe that one foul deed wiped out another . . .

He hadn't met the raiders returning to Massacre, so he guessed they must have returned by the easier route, down the Sycamore and along the Smoky Hill River itself. He turned his horse that way. He thought, 'They can't be more than half an hour ahead of me, an' they'll be goin' slow now. If I c'n catch up with 'em an' identify 'em, I'll turn 'em over to the military.'

He rode for less than five miles before he came upon them. They must have been very confident, for they had camped by the river's bank, and had lit a mighty big fire that illuminated the water for a hundred yards across.

By the sound of it, they had brought some liquor with them and they were drinking hard, celebrating their 'victory'.

Cheyenne didn't hesitate. He took his Colt out and held it against the saddle where it couldn't easily be seen. Then he rode up towards the fire.

He was still approaching, still unseen, when he saw the whole picture. There were only nine men in the party. They were the scum of the frontier, with a sprinkling of young, easily-led men among them. Fools and knaves,

27

Cheyenne thought, but all had stained their hands foul red with their appalling crime.

And even now they weren't through. Cheyenne's rage boiled over at the spectacle before him. The drunken, blood-lusting white men had been torturing an Indian prisoner.

When Cheyenne saw him, the red man was staked out on the ground just by the fire, and he could guess what had been done to him. The agent looked down into that face, and he knew that death would come to him at any moment now – what that red man had suffered was more than any man could stand and continue to live.

The prisoner seemed to see Cheyenne Joe before the others and his eyes lit up – just for a second there was the sparkle of life and hope in them, and then it began to die.

Cheyenne lifted eyes that were grey with misery, eyes that were sick from the sight before him. He rode his horse across the spread-eagled body of the dead brave, so that all could see him in the leaping firelight, and his voice rang with passion as he shouted: 'You murderin' swine, I'll see you all swing for this!'

And he was looking round quickly, looking from face to face, impressing on his memory their features so that he could ever more identify them with this unnecessary tragedy.

'What'n heck,' growled a bearded pioneer uneasily. 'Who's makin' a fuss 'cause we levelled things up with them damned redskins? It ain't murder to kill them varmints no more'n it's murder to kill a rattlesnake.'

There was a growl of approval at his word, the approval of men quick to find justification for what they knew to be excesses.

Cheyenne snapped, 'The army c'n decide that legal point.'

He stopped. Someone had moaned, out beyond the fringe of firelight. Then Cheyenne switched his eyes back from the darkness and looked at those evil, menacing faces that ringed him round. They were looking at each

other nodding . . . coming stealthily closer. A log exploded
on the fire, sending up a shower of sparks and a sheet of
sudden, dancing flame. By its light Cheyenne saw movement back among the bushes . . .

Now he wanted to be away. He knew he could identify
these desperadoes whenever required, and now it was
doubly urgent that he made all haste to the Cheyenne
camp. He kicked his horse suddenly, and it broke through
the ring of men, sending some back quickly with startled
oaths. He knew that the moment he turned his back on
them they would open fire on him because, drunk though
they were, they knew that their lives were forfeit while he
remained alive as witness to their crimes.

So he started to pull his horse backwards towards the
protective cover of the darkness, facing them with that
Colt in his hand.

And then that moan came again.

He could have spurred safely away at that moment,
because he had acted too swiftly for their drink-dulled
brains to anticipate him, but suddenly he knew he could-
n't leave this place without learning the origin of those
moans.

Again a log, dry from the hot summer's days, cracked
open with a sound like an explosion – so sudden it made
the men jump and turn apprehensively. While they were
still off their guard Cheyenne went spurring forward
across the ring of firelight.

He found the brush. Found more than one person lying
there in its cover. There was a man down among the leaves
and grasses, and he was holding a slight, struggling form;
he had a big, calloused hand clapped over the mouth to
prevent anything but a moan from coming through.

And Cheyenne saw it was a girl who was being held
down a prisoner – an Indian girl. And that other face that
was lifted towards him, swollen almost beyond recogni-
tion, above that Indian maiden, was the face of his old
adversary, the teamster.

Cheyenne pulled back his horse so that it reared high

above the pair. He saw the blank fear that registered on the brutal, distorted face below, saw the hope spring to the eyes of the Indian maiden at sight of him.

Then the girl pulled away from that hand and she cried, ' O Jo-shay, you have come to save me from these men who would torture me!'

And Joe Shay answered in Cheyenne, 'I will take you away, Blue Flower.'

It happened so quickly that the battered teamster hadn't time to get to his feet. One moment Cheyenne Joe was in his saddle the next he was dropping feet first out of it, and those feet were driving straight for the sagging body of the teamster.

The startled men back by the fire saw their companion trampled on, saw the Indian girl lifted and slung across the horse. They went for their guns, got them out and raised them to fire. But Cheyenne Joe wasn't there to be fired at – they couldn't see him. For he was holding on to his saddle from the far side, racing with his mount towards the darkness.

Someone spotted the trick and shouted, 'Get that hoss!' and lifted his rifle to shoot the animal down. But a revolver barked in time, and the rifleman bellowed with agony as a bullet tore into the muscle of his right arm. Cheyenne Joe had pulled off a lucky shot over the neck of his horse.

Next moment he was a fast-moving shadow in the darkness – and safe. He swung up into his saddle without slackening the speed of his mount. The girl was hanging on grimly, slung across in front of him. He grasped her lifted and turned her, shouted, 'Get your legs astride – we might have to do some hard ridin'!'

But the pursuit was feeble. By the time the men had found their horses they had nothing to chase except some echoes in the darkness, and being far from sober they made a poor job of it. In less than ten minutes Cheyenne knew they had nothing to fear, and he settled down to a very easy canter in order to let his mount recover from its recent burst of speed under double burden.

The moon gave them good light until well after midnight, when clouds came rolling down from Pikes Peak, leaving them in darkness. Cheyenne kept on as long as he could, but in the end he had to halt.

He dismounted, fumbled in his pack in the dark and gave the girl his blanket. She didn't want to take it, saying that Jo-shay should have it as of right. She was only Blue Flower, a simple Indian maiden, while wasn't he the greatest of the white men after the White Father in Washington?

He told the girl that it might be right for an Indian to have the comforts, but a white man gave them to his womenfolk. He kicked around a bush until he was sure there was no snake lurking there, and then he curled up among the leaves and promptly fell asleep.

He awoke at first light, and immediately went across to waken the girl. He was desperately anxious to rejoin the tribe without delay so as to prevent any further deterioration in relations between whites and the red peoples.

The girl was curled up snugly in the blanket, so that only her glossy black hair was to be seen. She must have unbraided it in the dark in order to give her greater comfort while she slept, and her hair flowed in rich, luxuriant masses over the vivid-striped Navajo blanket.

He stooped to waken her. Time was urgent, and she had had all the sleep he could allow. On an impulse he took the soft, silky hair between his strong brown fingers and gave it a little tug.

The effect was astonishing. The blanket heaved, then was thrown aside. Cheyenne, startled, saw a bare brown arm strike towards him, and there was a knife held in the hand, a glittering, curving Bowie that flashed in the brightening light.

He moved too late. The knife-point bit through the sleeve of his shirt, just below the left elbow. The weight of the thrust carried it on and through. There was a sickening shock of pain as the steel ripped through the muscle of his forearm – through it until it emerged and

31

dug into the ground below.

Off his balance, pinned to the ground by the agonizingly painful Bowie blade through his arm, Cheyenne Joe fell flat on his back, for a second helpless, at the mercy of his assailant.

And he looked up into fierce black vengeful eyes – the eyes of Blue Flower, the Indian maiden whom he had saved from his vicious, sadistic compatriots only a few hours before.

CHAPTER THREE

BLUE FLOWER!

For one second he could only gaze blankly up at the girl, and in that time she could have killed him if she had tried.

But in that second full wakefulness came to her, and with it doubt. Cheyenne saw the fierceness ebb from her handsome face, saw uncertainty replace it, and then horror.

He didn't know what it meant, not just then. All he knew was that her weight was still holding that Bowie knife through his forearm, and the agony of it was excruciating.

Without thinking, his reaction automatic to the acute pain, his right arm came over in a swift circle; it caught the girl on the shoulder and flung her away into the mesquite. Cheyenne rolled with the blow and plucked frantically at the knife through his arm. Then – even then in the midst of that blinding pain – he remembered that the point was in the earth, and to withdraw the knife through the forearm was to pull dirt into the wound.

With blood pouring in a little fountain from the entrance to the wound, he pulled the knife clear of the ground and wiped it with his bandanna before slowly easing it from the wound. It hurt, but he set his teeth grimly and completed his painful task.

And when the Bowie knife was out he looked at it and realized that it was his own.

He looked across at Blue Flower. She was crouching back in the mesquite, her big brown eyes watching him intently. There was horror in them at sight of the reddening sleeve with its cascade of blood pouring down through the cuff, but there was also fear – fear of reprisals to follow.

Wearily Cheyenne eased himself into a comfortable sitting position. He looked at his useless arm, and then called softly: 'Come and fix this wound, Blue Flower.' He understood now.

She crept towards him on all fours, like some frightened animal. She was mostly wild, anyway, Cheyenne thought. All the same, he didn't like to see it.

Cheyenne spoke to her.

'You took this knife out of my belt while we rode last night, didn't you?' he chided gently. Her eyes tremored a little. 'You don't trust any white man after what happened to you yesterday, do you, O Blue Flower?' The eyes dropped before his. 'Not even Jo-shay, who has always been the red man's friend? Not even me?' And somehow he felt hurt, because until now he had thought himself completely accepted by the red men that he laboured for.

She lifted those big brown eyes for a second, her lips parted slightly as if she would speak, and he saw the even whiteness of her teeth within. But then her eyes fell and she moaned without saying a word.

Cheyenne sighed. 'I don't blame you, Blue Flower. You saw last night what isn't good for any gal to see. I shouldn't have wakened you like that.'

He held out his wounded arm. He bore her no malice, but felt only a sorrow for her because of what she must have gone through to have made her like this.

'Come an' fix this,' he repeated; but she didn't move.

He tossed the Bowie knife towards her. She flinched, thinking at first that he was trying to hit her with the

34

weapon, and then she realized that that was not his intention.

'All right, Blue Flower,' he told her. 'You c'n hold on to my knife, if that helps.'

But the gesture seemed enough. She left the knife where it lay and came stumbling towards him. When she came up to him she knelt at his side and began to fumble at the bloodsoaked buttonhole to his sleeve, and he realized that she was trembling.

So he talked to her, softly, gently, soothingly. He told her what he thought of bad men, red and white; told her how he hated violence and war which caused suffering, and how always he worked to prevent strife between two peoples who should have been friends. And he stroked that soft, luxuriant mass of black hair, much as he would have stroked the mane of a terrified colt, and in time she stopped trembling and seemed reassured and to believe him.

She never spoke all the time she was attending to him, and after a time he fell silent and watched her nimble fingers as they cleaned the wound, staunched it by spreading spiders' webs to coagulate the blood around the knife-slit, and then bound it with his bandanna and some soft shirt material of her own.

When it was done they stood up. They had lost valuable time and now must be on their way. He went for his horse, which had remained saddled and bridled during the night in case of need for a swift getaway, then remembered the Bowie knife in the ground and sent Blue Flower back for it.

He told her to mount before him, and she climbed nimbly on to the horse. He swung up behind her, and urged his mount into a quick walk. He wished he could find another horse for Blue Flower, because they would make slow progress, both riding his horse, and he wanted speed.

After some time he felt Blue Flower stir before him. She didn't speak, but he felt her hands reach round for the sheath of his Bowie knife. Looking down, he saw her return the blade she had stolen during the night ride.

When that was done she turned to look ahead, and she never spoke.

And Cheyenne's heart jumped and filled with pleasure. It seemed that the girl no longer feared him, and that pleased him. He reached up and patted her shoulder and felt the warmth of her through the buckskin shirt. She never moved; never by any sign let him see that she had felt the little touch of approval.

And yet he was sure she, too, was pleased.

A day later they ran into a band of war-painted Indians and were captured and taken prisoner.

The warriors were resting on a grassy shelf above a bright little stream that sang a cheerful song as it splashed over the yellow pebble bed.

And they were Cheyennes.

They came running across the stream when they saw Cheyenne Joe and the Indian girl, but perhaps because the pair were obviously harmless they didn't look threatening. There were signs of war-paint on the fierce faces, but clearly this halt had been to give them chance to clean themselves up preparatory to riding into camp.

Cheyenne looked down from his saddle and saw that fresh scalps adorned the belts of many of the warriors.

His eyes sought the leader of the war-party. It was a minor chieftain who led them, but a man of importance within the tribe because he was also a member of the Warrior Council, which, even more than chieftains, dictated policy.

For a long time Cheyenne Joe had had his eye on the man, for he was a troublemaker. He was young and ambitious, and peace irked him.

Cheyenne had to think for a moment before remembering the chieftain's name. Then it came to him – White Fox. White, because he painted his face all white when he rode into battle, and Fox because of the cunning he was known to possess.

36

They were in overwhelming numbers, but Cheyenne spoke out bluntly: 'White Fox has broken the treaty with the paleface. White Fox has led his men into battle against the peaceful trader known as Luther and the settlers down from the trading post. Assuredly White Fox must have a good reason for this conduct.'

White Fox drew himself erect arrogantly. 'White Fox has a good reason. White Fox went with his men to get supplies, but Luther would not give them because we did not have the money yet.'

'What do you mean – you didn't have the money – yet?' demanded Cheyenne.

'The White Father in Washington is late in sending us the money he promised. We promised Luther to come and pay him with the dollars that you, Jo-shay, had said you would bring on your return.'

'And Luther said "no" to that proposition?' Luther would. He was a canny trader, and he knew it was less than a fifty-fifty chance that the Indians got the promised bounty for staying on their reservations.

'Luther said maybe red man never get bounty.' And then, according to White Fox, because they would not leave the post until they were given credit, Luther had tried to push them out. White Fox had grown angry.

'I killed him!' he growled suddenly, defiantly.

Cheyenne Joe watched him closely. He knew Mark Luther. Mark was too Indian-wise to lay hands on a Cheyenne chief and push him about. So he said, coldly: 'Did White Fox imagine that Mark Luther laid hands on him – because he wanted an excuse to put a scalp in his belt?'

White Fox said nothing, but his face grew stony because his word was being publicly doubted. Cheyenne sighed to himself. He felt that he was probably right; felt that White Fox had gone to make a quarrel and had been successful.

He kicked his heels into his horse's ribs, preparatory to riding away.

'We will talk on this again when we reach the camp of your people!' he threatened. 'You have broken the promise of chieftains greater than you, O White Fox, and they will surely mete out retribution!'

White Fox jumped forward at that and seized the head of Cheyenne's horse. His face was passionate with fury, yet even now he did not lay hands on the Indian agent. Cheyenne Joe had too many good friends within the tribe for him to try to harm him.

Arrogantly he declared that he, White Fox, was not afraid to answer for what he had done; and then, cunningly, he added: 'Maybe the Strong Hearts will forget the peace you have spoken of for so long when White Fox tells them that even the white men do not trust the promises of their White Father in Washington.'

'You will get your bounty,' promised Cheyenne Joe coldly. 'It is late, but it will come when your hands are taken from your scalping knives and you are at peaceful purposes again.'

White Fox was suddenly confident.

'Jo-shay went to bring in the bounty. Why does Jo-shay return with promises on his lips but with his hands empty?'

'Because,' Cheyenne Joe said truthfully, 'you killed people in defiance of the promises of your nation, and I came to have you hanged in consequence.'

White Fox and his followers stiffened with shock and hatred at his words; then the chieftain's eyes became part-lidded to hide the warm, molten venom in them while he said: 'White Fox does not believe the paleface. All palefaces are liars. If Jo-shay could have brought the bounty with him, he would have done so.' And then his eyes lit up as an idea came to him. 'Maybe Jo-shay wants to keep the bounty. Maybe Jo-shay has the red man's dollars and seeks to keep them all to himself!'

And suddenly, to the twisty mind of the cunning Indian, that seemed a reasonable conclusion. Suddenly he and his followers believed the theory that had come so glibly to his lips.

Cheyenne said: 'We'll talk that over when we reach camp. Maybe my friends in the tribe won't be so ready to believe that theory, White Fox.'

They set off, Cheyenne and Blue Flower in the midst of the Indians. It was a gesture, making Cheyenne a prisoner, an effort to save the arrogant young chieftain's face. And it didn't worry the agent at all. It was his intention to go to the Cheyenne camp, and he didn't mind travelling along with the war-party – so long as he got there in the end.

When they took the trail again, climbing and twisting among the little wooded hills that made the plain less flat than it appeared from the heights behind, Cheyenne's attention came abruptly to Blue Flower.

Somehow a change had come over her since their meeting with the Indians. Before she had seemed at ease, resting against him as they rode, but now she sat stiffly away from him, as if not wishing to touch any part of him with her body.

So after a time he spoke softly, so that only she heard him, and he said: 'O Blue Flower, why do you sit away from me? Have I offended you in any way?'

She hesitated, then turned so that he could look down into her lovely brown eyes. Brown? They seemed nearly black just then. And they were troubled. They looked at him, dropped before his gaze, then came stealing back. And then she turned and her head was bowed, and he had difficulty in catching the words she uttered.

'Jo-shay is a paleface. I can never forget that!'

Joe Shay would have spoken again on the subject, wanting to know the meaning of her words, but White Fox had seen them whispering together, and to his cunning mind whispering spelt danger towards himself, and he pushed his pony closer to hear them. Cheyenne saw the move and became silent, and after that, right until the moment they came into the Cheyenne camp, there was never opportunity again for them to speak alone together.

In his absence the laggards had joined the main body of the tribe, and now their tepees made a giant circle around the council lodge by the great council fire. All of three thousand people were there, all that were left of the great Cheyenne Nation, the finest fighters in Indian history.

White Fox tried to make something of a ceremony of his arrival with his 'prisoner,' but Cheyenne wasn't going to let himself appear in any poor light where the young chieftain was concerned. Instead he deliberately, publicly, humiliated him.

White Fox was riding proudly by his side. Cheyenne took his foot out of his stirrup, hooked it under the bent knee of the chieftain, and all in the same movement kicked upwards.

Caught off his balance, White Fox slipped on the smooth back of his saddle-less pony and suddenly disappeared under its belly. It was a trick often played by young braves upon each other, and now a howl of laughter greeted the downfall of the conceited young White Fox.

Cheyenne reined in his horse and said acidly: 'Why do you play, O White Fox? I thought you had made me your prisoner, but it seems you need someone to look after you.'

And then he walked his horse away from the discomfited war-party and approached the lodge of his friend, Chief Black Bear. Suddenly Blue Flower slipped from the horse and ran away among the tepees. Cheyenne watched her go, wondering what was in her mind. It wasn't easy to understand these Indian maidens—

Chief Black Bear, short, strong, built like the bear from whom he had received his name, raised his hand in salute.

'How!' he called. He didn't ask any questions of his friend, but when Cheyenne had dismounted he spoke outright to the chief.

'O Black Bear,' he told him, 'that Indian who is so well-named after the wily fox will bring trouble upon you. See his face now – see the hatred in it. He is planning to do harm to me – and to others!' And then softly he added: 'And maybe to you, too, O Chief!'

Black Bear grunted: 'White Fox wants war. Always he speaks of war. And what he says is to the liking of the young men, who live for war and for scalpings. White Fox will do anything to bring the Cheyenne people into war again!'

Cheyenne nodded grimly. 'White Fox has tried to bring war upon you – tried hard since he left the camp. And maybe this time he has succeeded.'

Black Bear looked hard at his white friend. 'What do you mean, O Jo-shay?'

'I mean that White Fox took out a party of braves and went scalping in Luther country. They have killed, by what I was told, upwards of a dozen people. You know what that means, Black Bear?'

Black Bear knew. He looked viciously across at the minor chieftain, standing within a growing circle of friends, talking to them. 'It means trouble – trouble for my people.' Black Bear was a realist. He knew that war-paint was little good against Winchesters, and now that the white man was securing these fine new repeater weapons the red man didn't stand a chance in battle.

Cheyenne stroke earnestly. 'I stopped the people of Massacre town from riding out to get revenge, O Black Bear. All except a few who sneaked off when I had ridden away. If White Fox is sent under escort for trial to Fort Tamberlin, along with others who took part in the raid, perhaps this matter will be settled without war between our peoples.'

Black Bear spoke. 'White Fox has broken the pledge between our peoples. White Fox will be handed over to the paleface for trial.' And then, watching that swelling group, he said abruptly: 'But it will not be easy.'

Cheyenne asked: 'Why?'

Black Bear sighed. 'See those braves who listen so eagerly to White Fox's serpent tongue.' Cheyenne looked across at the group. There must have been fifty men there

41

now, all listening eagerly and with excitement to the chieftain.

'All those braves,' said Black Bear, 'are Strong Hearts.'

'Oh!' said Cheyenne thoughtfully.

The Strong Hearts was the name given to the members of the Warrior Council – that body elected from the Cheyenne people to debate policy for the tribe. These Strong Hearts – the bravest, fiercest of the fighters – were all-powerful. They decided when a tribe should go to war or remain at peace, and when they had come to a decision it was for the chieftains to implement the policy.

Black Bear sighed. 'My people do not like this life in a reservation. Nowhere in the territory is the buffalo that we used to hunt, and there is little game, and my people go hungry even though it is high summer. They grow restless, and the moment you are out of camp, O Jo-shay, they begin to talk war. Only your presence has kept them quiet so long.'

There was a twinkle in his deep brown eyes as he said: 'If my people should ever find you like other white men, a schemer and full of guile and intent on your own interest, then assuredly there would be nothing to stop them and they would take up their pots of war-paint and sharpen their hatchets and ride to destruction against their hated white foes.'

Yet it was apparent that Black Bear could not believe that his white friend was like other palefaces whom he had met. Plainly Black Bear did not think that Cheyenne Jo-shay would ever betray his red friends.

'Within a couple of hours of your departure White Fox rode out on a hunting trip,' Black Bear told him. The Strong Hearts, with White Fox in their midst, were coming across to where they were standing by the Council Lodge. 'I was suspicious even then – it was a large hunting party, and the men in it were the hot-heads, those who would seek trouble.'

'They are trying to force the Cheyennes into war,' said the Indian agent softly.

'With your help, O Jo-shay, we will keep our people at peace,' he heard Black Bear say, and then the Strong Hearts were upon them.

White Fox, as a chief among warriors, was their spokesman. Into his voice came respect, for Black Bear was a mighty chief and one to be feared.

'O chief,' he said, 'there are many among us who would speak around the council fire. There is much that we would speak of, and it is in our hearts that we would speak of it now.'

Black Bear looked round the Strong Hearts. 'Is it your wish, too?' A growl of assent went up from the warriors. 'Then,' said Black Bear, 'let us hold council and hear what you have to say.'

At once a messenger was sent around the lodges to bring in the full council of Strong Hearts, while a ceremonial fire, unnecessary in that warm sunshine, was lighted outside the great Council Lodge that had needed the skins of over ninety buffalo to build it. As the warriors came up, they seated themselves in a great circle around the fire.

A whisper of the business in hand must have gone around the camp, for a great concourse of people came and stood at a distance to watch the proceedings. Cheyenne looked at them, but their impassive faces did not betray their thoughts. He wondered what they wanted, these people of the Cheyennes – did they hope for war arising out of this council, or peace?

Then he looked for Blue Flower, but he could not see her in that great throng. Cheyenne sat with the chiefs. When the assembly was all gathered, White Fox rose and stalked out into the open before the fire, and he lifted his voice so that all could hear, even the concourse behind the Warrior Council.

'I am White Fox,' he began proudly. 'I am so named because I am cunning and can see farther into the future than most men. And for long I have told you that the white man spoke with lies upon his lips, that he did not intend to keep his word to the red man. It has happened before, and I say it is happening again.

'We were promised many dollars if we would bury the hatchet and stay here within this miserable reservation. We have stayed here, but have we received the promised bounty?'

A growl went up from the Indians. It was a sore point with them that the promised payment was now well behind time.

'No, though it was promised for more than a moon ago, we are still without the money we need. And we must have that money, for without it we will starve here in the reservation. There is not enough game, not enough land for us, and we must buy corn and blankets and other things we need.'

He paused and looked deliberately at Cheyenne Joe. 'We shall never receive that bounty,' he said fiercely. 'We are being tricked. It is not the white man's intention to pay us. Even the white man himself says there will be no payment made to us.'

Just as deliberately Cheyenne called back: 'The white man whose scalp you carry at your belt, O White Fox?'

White Fox flung round, hands widespread and open. Suddenly he became an orator, explaining, persuading, justifying.

He had gone in the disgrace of his poverty, he and his friends, to buy needed provisions from the trader, Luther, he told them. And Luther, he declared fiercely, had despised them for a poor, worthless people. Luther had been so little certain that they would ever be able to pay him from the promised bounty that he had refused to lend them goods.

'So I killed him,' said White Fox suddenly. 'I am a Cheyenne, the mightiest of the tribes in the Indian Federation. And a Cheyenne kills when a man seeks to humble him.'

A savage shout of approval arose from the Indians around the fire, and it spread and was taken up by the throng beyond it.

Black Bear rose then, and held up his hand for silence. In cold, unemotional tones he said: 'O White Fox, it was the promise of our people that we would not raise our hands against the white man. You have done this – you have made yourself greater than the laws of the Cheyennes. Therefore you must pay the penalty for what you have done.'

A growl of disapproval went up. White Fox heard it, and it made him very confident. He had known in his heart that when the time came he would find the greatest of support for his actions within the tribe, no matter what he did against the white man.

But Black Bear went on speaking. 'To save our tribe from complete destruction, we made a pact with the white man. And the Cheyenne's word is good, and we must see that it remains good. If we are to break our promise to deliver up the wrong-doers in our midst, then assuredly evil will befall us.'

Joe Shay came up to his feet at that, nursing his throbbing, stiffened arm. 'If you do not give White Fox and his men over to me, O People, assuredly the military will come and take him from you and kill many in the process.'

White Fox jumped to his feet, and with him came a dozen or so of his followers. 'Let the soldiers try to take us! Do you think the Cheyenne nation will stand by and let them ride into our midst?'

And that was what Cheyenne Joe was afraid of. If it came to a show-down, and the army had to send an expedition to bring out White Fox and his followers from the Cheyenne camp, he knew that the moment the hated blue uniforms were seen every Cheyenne would charge into battle. And then the war would be on again.

No, he had to get White Fox away from the tribe, to stand his trial at a distance where his actions couldn't affect his people.

Black Bear stood forward again. 'The army will not come to this camp. And why, O White Fox? Because we will be true to our promise and will give you to Jo-shay to

45

take to Fort Tamberlin. Only that way can we keep our people from trouble.'

It was sense, but there were men among them who didn't want to listen to sense, and now they shouted against it. Cheyenne saw the Strong Hearts rising, their hands seeking weapons even now – he saw them beginning to split up into two factions.

And White Fox taunted: 'Come and take me, O Joshay!'

At that, wounded though he was, surrounded as he was by Cheyennes, Cheyenne Joe walked forward until he was within a couple of yards of the arrogant young chieftain. He spoke, and his voice was raised just as White Fox's had been raised, so that all could hear.

'You have brought tragedy upon your tribe, O White Fox. For assuredly there must be retribution for what you have done. You have broken the promise of your people, and for that there will be suffering.'

He paused, then dramatically pointed his finger. 'But are you a woman that you would let others suffer for the follies you have committed, or are you a man to stand the consequences yourself?'

Cheyenne Joe knew that in boldness was his strength. To show weakness now would mean the loss of everything he had worked for – and perhaps of himself, too.

And it seemed that his boldness would win the tribe over to him, for now men who had gone to join White Fox's party considered again and detached themselves from his supporters. In a moment White Fox's band had dwindled to a handful, and it seemed that the Indian agent was gaining the ascendant.

And then someone stepped out from among the gathering behind the Warrior Council and challenged the wisdom of his words – aye, and the justice of them. Challenged him and defeated him.

And the name of that person was Blue Flower.

CHAPTER FOUR

THE SNAKES

Suddenly she was standing there, afraid to speak before the great ones of her tribe, and yet daring to do it because of the things she had seen and the way she had suffered.

He heard her voice, and it was without the music normally within it – it was strained with passion and intermittently broke as she grew too emotional.

'Will the white man hand over to the Cheyennes those palefaces who killed my people last night – who attacked while we slept and showed mercy neither to women nor to the babes in their arms?'

There was a shocked silence from the Indians at that. They did not know yet of the slaughter in Sycamore Creek. So Blue Flower told them about it. Told how they had gone peacefully to camp, on the way to join their tribe. How they had pitched their tepees within the limits of the Cheyenne territory, in a pleasant valley that had looked peaceful and secure, but had become the grave for most of them.

She told of the awakening in the night, when guns barked suddenly, and heavy bullets tore through the buffalo walls of their lodges and wounded and killed as they stood up from their beds.

She told of the slaughter as her wounded menfolk went bravely out to fight and were hacked down by a savage enemy, and while she spoke of it the faces of her audience hardened and the mercy went from their hearts.

'They killed my people,' she called passionately. 'If it is right that we hand over our men to justice, it is yet but right that they give to us the men who committed this deed against my family!'

A shout went up at that from every throat. It seemed right to those Cheyennes. At once men stepped forward from the Warrior Society.

'Until the white man hands over their miscreants, we will not give White Fox over to Jo-shay!' they shouted, and a mighty roar of approval came from their savage throats.

Cheyenne Joe stood, his heart despairing. He could see the reasoning behind the Indians' argument, but he knew it wouldn't count where the white man held court. He knew that if the Cheyennes didn't surrender their criminals, then the army would come against them with all the might they possessed. Scalping white settlers and the trader was a crime that could only be expunged by the death of the murderers.

Cheyenne tried to reason with them even now, though he knew he was fighting a lost cause.

'White Fox killed those Cheyennes as surely as he killed Luther and the other settlers whose scalps he carries. If he hadn't gone to war the white man would not have retaliated by riding against peaceful Indians.'

White Fox came pushing forward through the excited throng that had closed about the solitary white man. 'So you knew about the killing of our people, O Jo-shay – yet you spoke only of the white man's losses, not the red man's!'

He wheeled and began to harangue the crowd, trying his hardest to turn them against this one white man whom they respected almost as a god.

'This Jo-shay,' he shouted, 'he is like other white men, speaking with a tongue that is forked like the serpent's, saying only what he wants us to believe, and not telling us all. Who is it who has kept us quiet in our restlessness, telling us that the White Father would be sending the bounty any day now? And who has still to show us the first silver dollar that is rightfully ours because we have come to live in this small, gameless reservation?'

He spread his hands wide and eloquently. 'It is Jo-shay. And I say this Jo-shay is a trickster like his brother whites. I say that he knows we will never get the bounty – because he has taken the Cheyennes' money for himself!'

Black Bear came forward while the crowd gasped at the bold words directed against the man who had always been regarded as their greatest friend. Black Bear knew his paleface friend too well to listen to such talk.

'This I do not believe,' he retorted. 'My life is forfeit if our friend, Jo-shay, is a serpent as White Fox says. I say that White Fox has the cleft tongue of the snake, and I tell you to guard against his lying tongue because he would bring disaster on the tribe.'

And then Cheyenne Joe had his say. He stepped forward, hand upraised for silence. 'The bounty is in Massacre town. I will bring it to you within three days – maybe four because the way is rough and stony for a covered wagon.' He looked at the Strong Hearts, pressed so closely to him now. 'If I bring in the bounty, thus keeping the promise of the White Father in Washington, will you keep your promise and hand over these bad men among you for justice?'

'And those bad white men?' parried an elder of the tribe.

'They,' promised Cheyenne, 'will die. I know them, every one. I will follow them and hand them over to justice—'

'And if the white man is less quick to hang his own kind?' – he was a grim old sceptic, that elder with the wrinkled, mahogany-coloured face.

'Then,' said Cheyenne simply, 'I will go and kill them with my own hands.'

Black Bear stepped up to Cheyenne's side and put an

arm affectionately round his shoulders. He faced his people, and said: 'My white brother is a man among men, and he will do as he says. Always Jo-shay has spoken with the tongue of truth, and this time is no different. Let us do as he says: Let us live at peace until he comes with the bounty, and then let us talk again on these matters that are like sores in our bosom.'

White Fox heard the approving murmurs, and again he came jumping forward, and now his eyes had lost a little of their confidence. He had been sure, even before he started on the war trail, that he would be able to sway the Cheyennes to his way of thinking, but this Indian agent was formidable – always he spoke to get the people to do as he said.

So now White Fox shouted: 'Do not listen to his lies! He seeks only to escape from us so that he can live and enjoy the money he has taken from us. If he goes, we will never see him again.'

Cheyenne spoke coolly in reply. 'White Fox nurses anger because I tipped him from his horse.' Someone laughed at the memory of that undignified somersault. 'I did it to show my contempt for this killer of old men and slaughterer of women. And again I will show my contempt for him. Let him select half-a-dozen Strong Hearts. Give them food that they can accompany me. I will lead them to the wagon in which is contained the bounty. And if I fail—'

'You dare not fail,' shouted White Fox savagely, and he called half a dozen names, and Cheyenne knew they were the names of savage advocates of war, and they would kill him if he failed to lead them to the commissioner's wagon.

And even as he thought of it, he remembered the dead Kentuckian, and the words he had uttered back there in the shadows by the Red Eye. A stab of uneasiness assailed him, because if the commissioner proved false to his employers, the United States Indian Office, then the consequences could be very serious to him, Joe Shay.

In all his relations with the Cheyenne, this was the

tightest predicament that Joe Shay had ever been in. These events had come to disturb the Indians and to cause them to forget all that he had done for them.

Black Bear took his right hand between his own. 'No matter what happens,' he said, 'I will work to keep my people at peace. It is better so. Have we not suffered enough from war?' And then he added gently, to his old companion of the hunting trails, 'And always, no matter what men tell me, I shall believe in my white friend, Jo-shay.'

Cheyenne Joe didn't speak. He went across to his horse. Someone filled his bottle and gave him some parched corn and dried meat, sufficient to sustain him over the next two or three days. Then he mounted, and rode slowly, regretfully out through the opening in the circle of tepees. Six fierce Strong Hearts rode closely after him – and all six, he knew, hated him and would be glad to do him harm.

Anger beat in his breast because of the fools who were intent on their own destruction. And then he turned, his heart aching for a last sight of Blue Flower. He bore her no ill will for upsetting his plans. She had been brought up in a state of primitive barbarity, and her reaction to what she had suffered wasn't beyond understanding.

But she wasn't there to see him ride through the tepees. He couldn't see her among the silent people who saw them set off – silent, yet as many were hostile towards him now because of the news they had learned, as there were forebearing.

A hundred yards outside the camp, Cheyenne turned for a last look. He saw the great congregation still watching after them through the gap in the circle . . . and then his eyes switched up the long curving line of tepees and he saw a solitary figure between two distant lodges.

Blue Flower!

And even from that distance he felt sure that the girl wept, but whether for him or for her dead family he didn't know. He shrugged. It would be for her dead, of course.

Indian girls didn't think much of white men, not girls like Cheyenne's Blue Flower. And he sighed, because he liked the brown-eyed Indian maiden, and he wanted her to like him in return.

Cheyenne was impatient and would have ridden through the night, but suspecting a trick, suspicious that he would give them the slip during the hours of darkness, the Strong Hearts ordered camp before the sun was completely down. Cheyenne Joe realized then that he was truly a prisoner – and realized that it would be as well for him that Commissioner Pengelly was waiting with the bounty.

Later next day, they came climbing up to the flats west of distant Massacre, upon which the immigrant camp had been pitched only five days before. They rode up a wooded defile, so that they came out very suddenly upon the open plain.

And it was empty. There wasn't a wagon in sight, only the marks of wheels that had turned and turned, and left only a confused mass of tracks that gave no story to anyone.

There was a man among the Strong Hearts who was known as Mountain Lion, and he was the leader of the party. When he saw that the plain was empty he spurred swiftly up to Cheyenne, and already his hand was on his scalping knife.

'It is as White Fox said, there is no wagon awaiting you.'

Cheyenne snapped, 'Maybe they pulled back into town.' One wagon wouldn't camp out here alone. When the immigrant train pulled out probably the commissioner had ordered them closer to Massacre in order to find greater safety.

He pulled his horse round, an automatic movement to one whose actions followed close upon thought. But Mountain Lion was there in front of him, barring his way.

'You think Mountain Lion is a child to swallow such a story?' the Strong Heart asked contemptuously. 'If we went with you would the white men let us come out of their village alive?'

Cheyenne looked round. The braves were all close up to him now their eyes watching him. And there was no mercy in them. On the contrary, there was a warm little gleam in their brown eyes, as if they mentally anticipated something enjoyable – like killing a man.

The brave known as Mountain Lion sat suddenly back on his horse. He had three eyes. Then Cheyenne saw the red rim and realized what it was, and straightway went rolling out of his saddle.

He was just beginning to fall when he heard the rifle that had fired the bullet through Mountain Lion's forehead. Then a volley crashed out and lead came whistling in among the braves.

They forgot Cheyenne Joe and dug their bare heels into their ponies and went racing for the cover of the defile. Two gained the trees without being hurt, but the other three were shot from their ponies and were either dead or dying in the long dry grass.

Cheyenne had fallen on his bad arm, and the pain was excruciating for a few moments. When the firing ended he raised his head cautiously, Colt in hand, for though he had virtually been prisoner to the Strong Hearts they had not attempted to take his gun away from him.

Some men were riding up. They seemed to be settlers or men from the town, but he didn't recognize any of them as they drew nearer.

They advanced suspiciously, their guns raised against him. Cheyenne rose, replacing his Colt in its holster. The men rode in quicker after that. Two detached themselves and went after his horse, which had run away in fright, but the other three came right up to Cheyenne. They seemed to recognize him and sight of him didn't altogether please them, apparently. He had an impression that they were suddenly a little uneasy, as if not sure that what they had done would gain approval.

Cheyenne said, 'Thanks, pards. You don't know it, but

you just saved my life.'

The rough, bearded men exchanged quick, relieved glances. 'Sure, sure, that's why we opened up on them varmints,' said one of the men hastily, but it didn't kid the agent.

He went across and took his horse as it was brought up. He had difficulty in mounting because of his stiff arm, but he got into the saddle and faced the settlers on equal terms.

Cheyenne said dispassionately. 'You were out huntin' for Injuns, aimin' to kill any on sight.' So much for his attempts to keep the people from retaliating in consequence of White Fox's depradations. 'You saw some Injuns an' you didn't inquire if they was up to anythin' mean, an' you just opened up on 'em.'

'Wal, what if we did?' That rough, scrub-faced settler wasn't ashamed of what he had done. 'We went up to Luther country an' saw what Injuns did up there. So we reckoned to wipe out any we caught outside the reservation.'

Cheyenne sighed. 'I wouldn't have let you go Injun huntin' if I had known, but – wal, you came just in time. Them critters sure reckoned to take the hair off my head, I guess.'

Then he remembered the commissioner's wagon. He questioned the men, but they were from a valley distant from the town and didn't know anything about the immigrant train that had passed through or of Commissioner Pengelly and his bodyguard.

Cheyenne left them, first making sure that the four fallen Indians were dead. He felt again that depression as he left the little battlefield. He had a feeling that he was to see many more Cheyenne dead before this trouble was over.

Trouble . . . Those two fleeing Strong Hearts would ride back to the Cheyennes, and would tell the Warrior Council that Jo-shay had lied – that there was no commissioner with his wagon-load of money, only white men with

54

rifles that killed from an uncanny distance.

He shrugged disconsolately. It was all over now, this friendship with the Cheyennes. Their respect for him had gone, and if they met him again they would regard him as an enemy more bitterly than most other white men.

He sighed. There were many whom he liked in the tribe – especially brave Black Bear, the best friend he had ever known. And there was Blue Flower. He had seen her around the Cheyenne camps before, and had liked her, and in the two days he had been with her after rescuing her from the murdering band of whites he had found his liking for her deepening.

In the Red Eye he secured a little more information. A man came forward who said he had seen the commissioner's wagon pull out with the immigrants. That information puzzled the Indian agent, for the immigrants would be striking north very soon, and that was away from Cheyenne territory. And he wondered why the commissioner had pulled out after it had been agreed that he would stay near to Massacre until Cheyenne's return.

Commissioner Wade Pengelly was a man to watch, the more so because of the charm which beguiled when he was around, Cheyenne thought grimly.

He went back of the bar with Andy Coan, into a tiny room that was filled with the bric-a-brac of a New York parlour and which looked out of place here in the crude West. And Cheyenne told him what had happened.

'There's goin' to be war?' And Coan's fat face looked grim. He was too old a man to enjoy skirmishes with the Indians.

Cheyenne shrugged. 'What do you think? No bounty – an' four of their men killed from ambush? I reckon White Fox will have all the Strong Hearts with him an' will come a-ridin' the war trails within a day.'

'So?'

'So I'm goin' to write some letters,' Cheyenne told him. 'I want warnin' to get through to Fort Tamberlin, an' I want a telegram to inform Washington that in consequence of their damn fool dilly-dallyin' with that bounty they've caused another Injun war. If they'd sent the money up when they promised, the Injuns would never have got restless like this.'

Andy Coan said drily: 'From what you say about Commissioner Pengelly, it seems he'd have got away with the bounty last month just as easily as this.'

'Yeah, I suppose so,' agreed Cheyenne heavily. The Indian Office was stiff with dishonest servants. He took the pen and paper that Andy offered him and then said: 'It might all be a false alarm, Andy. Black Bear an' his friends might keep the peace. I know he'll try.'

'But in your heart you don't think he'll be successful?' Cheyenne shook his head. 'Then,' said Andy, 'we'd better figger on war breakin' out within the next day or so.'

'All right. Get me some good men to go ridin' out into the country to warn people what to expect. If the Cheyennes strike, they mustn't catch our people unawares, like they did in Luther country.'

Our people— A little while ago he had called the Cheyennes his people, but they weren't. When the time came, when it came to war between the white and the red men, his people was the white race and his place was by their side.

He would have to fight, hating it though he did, against his old friends.

Andy Coan went out into the bar and Cheyenne Joe, writing, heard his voice as he made the announcement of another Indian war. There was a lot of scuffling of chairs after that, and a rising hum of excited talk. Then men went clumping out on to the board walk and took to their horses and went out to their families.

When he had finished writing, Joe sealed up the letters and went out into the saloon in search of Andy. The Red Eye proprietor was leaning his fat stomach against a bar that was deserted of customers, and his round face was mournful at the contemplation of the future. He was a quiet, gentle man, and hated the thought of strife.

Cheyenne gave the letters over to him, and Andy waddled out in search of two smart riding youngsters who would deliver the mail. As he went out he gave his opinion that Fort Tamberlin wouldn't be able to help them much.

'Reckon they won't have the men to spare,' he opined. 'Since the peace treaty with the Injuns they've reduced the garrison strength to a third what it used to be.'

Cheyenne nodded. He'd heard that, too.

'We've just got to fight this battle alone until they bring troops in from the East,' he said. Then he went out to his horse, mounted and rode off to the flats where the immigrants had camped.

It took him several hours of scouting around before he was sure that the wagon had followed out on the trail of the immigrants. But if that were so, where was it going? Because ten miles along the trail and the immigrants would head north-west, and that was away from Cheyenne territory.

It wasn't any good following along those tracks that day, because it was getting dark and his horse was weary. He himself felt pretty jaded, too, for his arm felt on fire again after that fall on it, and he seemed in a fever.

When he rode back to the Red Eye – doing brisk business once again – he looked so fatigued that Andy came round the bar to him. Cheyenne just mumbled: 'I'll be all right with some sleep, Andy. Guess it's this arm that's makin' me like this.'

But next day he was quite ill, and they fetched a doctor in from Saw Trees to dress his wound. For that reason he was never able to follow the tracks of that immigrant train with which Commissioner Pengelly and his escort had travelled.

For two days after his return from the Cheyenne agency, refugees came pouring into Massacre, fleeing before the warring Cheyennes.

The Indian agent stood out on the veranda along with others to watch the dismal procession. At first a few riders came spurring in to say that hundreds of braves had swept all along the range south of Luther country, killing, pillaging, and destroying as they rode.

Then came the fortunate settlers who had managed to get away before the fury of the Indian avalanche fell upon them.

They came in carts and wagons, or mounted two or three up on farm horses and mules. And they brought with them a few pathetic possessions that they treasured or thought they might need, and these were tied to their vehicles or bundled behind the riders. On the carts the women and children sat on top of the bundles, and the small ones thought it was a wonderful adventure and they much preferred it to their normal day.

Then, after the refugees, came the wounded, injured in the fight against the invaders. Cheyenne looked out on to heads wrapped in bloody bandages, on drooping, pain-racked bodies that swayed in the saddles. He saw men who would never walk on two legs again, and men who would go armless if they were fortunate enough to survive the primitive frontier surgery.

It made him sick, and he turned to go away. He was turning when he heard a soft voice: 'They're your friends done that, Mister Shay. Them good friends you was always talkin' about.'

They had been quiet before on that veranda, those patrons of the Red Eye, but at those soft-spoken, malice-edged words a deathly stillness came over them, too. For this was fighting talk.

Joe Shay came back to face the speaker. He saw a man smaller than himself, with a black beard and face above it that looked curiously pale. And brown, hooded, unpleasant eyes looked covertly through short lashes at him – while the man kept a hold on the butt of his revolver, as if ready for action at the slightest movement from Cheyenne Joe.

Cheyenne said tiredly: 'Yeah, they were my friends. Maybe they could have gone on bein' friends, too, but for that damn' fool Government holdin' on to the bounty they promised 'em.'

The man said deliberately: 'Once an Injun, always an Injun.' And if he had said: 'Once a killer, always a killer' his meaning would have been the same. 'There'll never be peace with them varmints in the country,' he added emphatically, and at that, there was a savage approving growl from the listeners.

Cheyenne walked away without saying more. He felt depressed and defeated. All his efforts to promote peace between reds and whites had been sabotaged by a tardy bounty and some restless, mistrustful Strong Hearts. He felt he wanted to keep out of arguments – all he wanted was to lie up in some quiet place and get his arm better.

All during the night people were riding in, so that Massacre was jammed with fugitives by morning light. And as they came they each contributed to a picture of the battle raging out to the west of them.

It was a story of sudden, savage forays by superbly mounted Indians, of farms blazing and men dying as they fought to save their families and precious possessions – of a few somehow managing to get away and spread the warning.

And then, all within half an hour, two riders came in with frightening information.

The first told them that the Shoshones had broken out from their reservation and had joined the Cheyennes in this insurrection. 'The Snakes,' thought the agent, perturbed, 'fightin' with the Cheyennes.' That was astonishing news, for the Shoshones – or Snake Indians – were traditional enemies of the Cheyennes.

Andy Coan knew what was in his mind. 'If the Snakes ride with the Cheyennes, you c'n bet in no time the Crows, Blackfoot Injuns, an' Dakota men will be out with 'em, too.'

Cheyenne said: 'If that happens, Andy, nothing can stop 'em until we cross the Mississippi.'

The second rider told them that a mighty horde of mixed Cheyenne and Soshone were within eight miles of Massacre.

CHAPTER FIVE

THE TELEGRAM

He spoke of a terrifying wave of Indians out on the western plains; and the way he described it there must have been a thousand out there, with reinforcements racing up every hour.

He was an exhausted man, on an exhausted horse, but the moment he had delivered his warning he set off again eastwards, towards the Smoky Hill River, and more than anything it spoke of the terrifying sight he had witnessed out on the prairie. It also indicated his opinion of the chances of Massacre to stand up to the avalanche successfully.

It had been unexpected, this sudden threat to the little frontier town, and no defence organization had been established. Able-bodied men had taken their rifles and gone riding out to help where they were needed, but there were no leaders and there had been no plan of action concerting all their efforts.

So now Andy Coan stood out on the veranda of his saloon and shouted to people to listen to him. In a few minutes there was a great gathering in the street, comprising every man and woman then in the town.

Andy shouted: 'Ef we don't use our heads, we're all gonna lose our scalps. Them Injuns is eight miles away – maybe less by now. Ef they come to Massacre – an' there's nothin' out there to stop 'em now – we couldn't hold this place for an hour. They'd burn us out – they'd shoot flamin' arrows on to the buildin's, an' they're so dry they'd go up in a flash.'

'What're we goin' to do?' someone shouted from the frightened, swaying crowd beneath him.

'We must go back down the Smoky River,' Andy shouted. 'The women an' children, the old an' the sick must leave immediately. The men must fight a rearguard action to protect them. Go an' get all the food an' ammunition you want, but do it quickly. Be out of this town, you women an' children, within five minutes, else you might never make Fort Tamberlin alive.'

Fort Tamberlln! Cheyenne Joe wheeled in astonishment. That was a hundred-and-twenty miles to the east of them. Did Andy think the whites would be driven all that way back – or that in a race, hampered by wagons containing women and children, they could win against the swift-riding Indians?

And then he thought: 'Andy's right. Now the Shoshones have thrown in their strength with the Cheyennes, there's nothin' to stop 'em until an army is sent out.'

The crowd broke up, rushing frantically to do as wise old Andy Coan said. Men went into the stores and came out carrying all the food they could lay their hands on, and there wasn't a man there who bothered to ask for payment for it. Then one by one the wagon horses were whipped up and went careering eastwards out of the town, women holding the reins, children clinging and calling goodbyes to their fathers and older brothers.

Gradually the town became quieter as the long procession of close on eighty wagons and carts snaked away down the yellow trail that led to the Smoky Hill River and the east.

Cheyenne had saddled his horse with difficulty; he'd got a Sharps rifle from Andy and was now trotting out on the western trail along with the other fighting white men.

At first they had about forty men in their party, but as

they rode westward more and more men came riding up to join them and bring them news of the fighting.

All evidence pointed to this being a very serious uprising, but what was most disturbing was the astonishing speed with which the Indians were sweeping through the countryside. As it was they were less than two miles from Massacre when they sighted the vanguard of the Indian horde.

It was a sight to depress them. Far out at the end of the flats was a wooded gorge that led into the hills. From it suddenly they saw riders emerging, pennants streaming from their lances, showing that they were Indians. The white men reined, the better to watch the Indian advance.

Within a couple of minutes there was an army of mounted men out there on the plain, with hundreds more streaming into view from the gorge. Cheyenne thought: 'We don't stand much chance of holding them back.' Andy Coan had been right; there was no defending Massacre against a horde like these.

A leader had been elected among the men. He was a well-known Indian fighter by the name of Gregory Bose, a spare, middle-aged man renowned for his sagacity. Now he started to give orders.

Their small force would be overwhelmed if they were caught out here on the plain. He ordered them back into the rougher country on the edge of the town, and he told them this was to be long-range fighting for them.

'We've got to hold 'em back from them wagons of women an' children,' he explained shortly. 'Fight a delayin' action so that they c'n get through until help rides out to meet 'em.'

It was to be a race, and the wagon train could only hope to win through if the men were successful in keeping back the Indian masses.

'We've got good weapons, better than the Injuns,' Bose told them. 'Use 'em intelligently. Fire the moment they are near enough for you to kill a man or hoss. But before they catch up with you, get on your hosses an' fall back.'

He divided the force into three parties, so that they could leap-frog each other in retiring – always there was to be one party covering the retreat of the others.

They went back into the cover of the broken country. One party dismounted, while the others took up covering positions a hundred yards back. Cheyenne, in spite of his wounded arm, was in the first party to meet the Indians.

They had seen the mounted whites and were streaming in mad fury across the plain to attack them. They were mostly Cheyennes, the Indian agent saw, though there were some Snake Indians among them.

Some of the men with good rifles, like new Winchesters, opened fire when the Indians were four hundred yards away. For all the effect it had, those bullets might have been gentle pattering raindrops. The Indians came screaming on without any slackening of pace. Then the other rifles took up the tale, and their harsh, crackling voices spoke, and this time they saw braves topple and fall from their ponies.

But still the Indians came on.

When they were a hundred yards away, someone shouted: 'Fall back – quick!'

They all jumped for their horses and want racing back towards the town. As they rode through the second line of defenders they heard the crackle of rifle fire all around them; then they were up with the third line of crouching defenders – saw them lift their heads and come into action. And then they were a hundred yards back and dismounting, throwing themselves down behind cover and preparing to open fire when it was their turn.

Cheyenne saw the second line of defenders jump for their horses, no more than fifty yards ahead of the nearest war-painted warriors. Then he pressed trigger as the invaders came within range of his gun.

The tactics were highly successful. Unable to come to grips with the white man because of his cunning leap-frog tactics, the Indians drew away and went circling in a mighty mass out on the flats while they debated the situation.

Bose came riding through to them at that. 'Sneak away,' he ordered. 'Let's get right through Massacre an' cover the trail alongside the Smoky.' On the open ground east of the town there would be no holding back these hard-riding Indians.

They pulled out quietly, keeping to cover, and when they were safely out of sight galloped along the dusty trail into the town again. As they were riding through, a compact mass of sweating men and lathered beasts, someone shouted, 'There's Andy Coan – an' Bill Phelan!'

The two old men had come running to the door of the store as the cavalcade came thundering through. Cheyenne pulled out of the throng as he saw his old friend still there in the town. He shouted, 'What're you waitin' for, Andy?'

But his fat friend just waved vaguely and then went running back into the store again. Cheyenne took it to be a signal of dismissal and began to walk his horse after the others.

He saw a horse tied to the side of the store and was a little reassured. At least the men had planned some way of retreat, whatever they were up to. But Andy Coan and the old storekeeper didn't follow immediately.

They trotted across the open land east of the town, to where the trail crossed the river and took up again along the south bank. There was a ford here, though a daring man could swim his horse at many points above and below the place and hope to beat the rushing, mountain torrent.

Greg Bose got them all across on to the south bank, then he sent them in parties for miles up stream as well as down. The river was a fine natural barrier, and if they behaved intelligently they could use it to hold back the Indians for many hours – and many hours meant so many more miles nearer to safety for the convoy of wagons.

Bose's instructions were brief. 'Shoot any varmint that tries to cross the river. But if some sneak across in force, fall back on to the main party an' give us warning.' Once let their line of retreat eastwards be cut off and they would be annihilated.

Cheyenne and the remainder of the party, mostly wounded like himself, were left by the ford to act as reserves, ready to be rushed in any direction where danger threatened. He kept gazing towards Massacre, wondering why the two old men didn't leave the place and come riding up to them while they had chance. Finally he could stand it no longer, and he asked Bose if he could go back towards the town and see what the men were up to.

'Them Injuns will be inside Massacre within minutes,' he told his leader. 'That looks like 'em now, movin' around among the scrub. Andy an' Bill won't stand a chance with one hoss between 'em.'

Greg Bose was uneasy. 'They shouldn't have stopped behind,' he agreed. 'All right, Joe, you go out, but don't get cut off because we need every rifle we've got now.'

Cheyenne put his horse to the ford and went riding quickly through the water. Once on the north bank, he dug his heels into his horse and raced towards the town.

But he was still a quarter of a mile away from it when he saw the spearpoint of the Indian attack come racing in. He reined, with a groan. Whatever they were doing, the two old timers had left escape till too late.

He stiffened in his saddle. A big, lumbering horse, heavily burdened, had emerged from the huddle of buildings at the east end of the town. Fat little Andy Coan was sitting in front, while behind, facing the horse's tail, was old Bill Phelan. And Bill was calmly firing a rifle into the nearest of the Indians.

All in one second it seemed to Cheyenne Joe that the town was alive with eager, looting Indians.

And the next it was blown sky high.

There was a low, rumbling roar, and then it seemed that a giant finger came pushing up through the centre of the town, lifting buildings before sending them tottering against others – and then the town collapsed like a pack of cards. While the startled Indians were trying to understand what had happened, the two old-timers made good their escape.

They rode up to where Cheyenne, a tight grin on his lips, awaited them. The two old men were looking very pleased with themselves. Andy called, 'We sure shook the feathers off'n a few braves that time, Joe.'

And old Bill Phelan took a long shot and knocked more feathers off a distant, unsuspecting brave.

Cheyenne called, 'That was good work, you old fire-eaters.' Yes, even at the cost of a town anything that harassed these Indians and reduced their strength was worth while. This surprise would make them more cautious, and cautious men didn't advance so fast.

He shouted, 'Look out, they're after you!' For a column of vengeful Indians had come wheeling round the shattered, burning town and were racing headlong towards them.

Cheyenne covered the retreat of the slow old horse with its double burden, picking off the advancing Indians as coolly as if he were shooting in a turkey contest. Then they came within range of Gregory Bose and his party's guns on the south bank, and the unexpected burst of fire was so withering that it sent the Indians careering suddenly away and gave the trio chance to walk through the ford.

Bose called, 'Was that some of your rot-gut that exploded, Andy? I always said it was brewed from gunpowder.'

Bill Phelan cackled, 'Nope. It was some spare kegs of powder, Greg. We fixed 'em in my cellar an' laid a short train an' waited for them varmints to come ridin' into town.'

Neither he nor Andy Coan seemed at all perturbed at having lost their businesses. But then these old-timers had seen it happen so often in their lives that they could take reverses philosophically.

They sat on the south bank and watched the town blaze, while the Indians massed out on the plain and planned their next move. Cheyenne looked at the sky. Another four hours before darkness. It wasn't likely that the Indians would attack after dark, and if they could last out for the next four hours it gave the wagon train chance to rest up for the next day's flight.

Some time later a body of Indians tried to force the ford while others of their number made the attempt to swim the river farther downstream. It proved an expensive attack, and the Indians were quickly thrown back in disorder, leaving the river stained with the blood of themselves and their horses.

After that they made no attempt to cross the Smoky at this point. Indians weren't persistent fighters. If they found themselves balked at one point, they immediately rode off in search of easier prey.

Now they watched while party after party went riding into the hills north of the town. They would devour the land like locusts, Cheyenne thought, and there wouldn't be a living white man within hundreds of square miles by nightfall.

Shortly after noon the following day the white men lost the ford and had to retreat quickly down-river. During that hot morning, lying there all along the river bank, men kept riding up from the south. They'd heard of the stand that was being made and they had come to join in it.

The story they told was of raging Shoshone Indians devastating even as far as fifty miles south of the Smoky, almost down to the Arkansas River. All in the back country were wagon trains heading for the Smoky Hill River trail and the security of the distant Fort Tamberlin.

And then the Shoshones came riding in from the south, turning their defences and exposing them to deadly danger.

Cheyenne Joe was watching the Cheyenne force across the river, which had been left to watch the defending white men, when suddenly heavy firing broke out only a hundred yards or so up river from him. Along with others he jumped for his horse.

He was mounting, when fifty war-painted braves came screaming out from cover, war shields raised in triumph at seeing the startled palefaces. They came hurtling up to the river, and their war whoops attracted the attention of the Cheyennes on the north bank who immediately came racing down to the ford again.

The white men beat off the Shoshones, though for a time there was savage hand-to-hand fighting. Cheyenne rode in, Colt blazing. He was handicapped when it came to the in-fighting because of his bandaged arm, but he laid about him with his empty rifle and knocked one brave off his mount under their trampling hoofs.

The revolvers of the white men were too devastating at close quarters, and after a brief skirmish the Snake Indians pulled out and raced away. That was always Indian warfare – a quick attack, then retreat at no less speed. And they weren't cowardly tactics, as some whites supposed; the strategy of Indian warfare was based upon speed and agility, and the United States army knew to its cost how effective it could be. Unfortunately the attack lasted long enough to permit the Cheyennes to ride through the ford. Greg Bose saw the leaders of a big party of Indians just emerging from the water and he shouted to the white men to retire in order along the trail.

It meant deserting their comrades: strung out higher along the river bank, but there was nothing else for it. They never saw any of them alive again.

Fighting a rearguard action was difficult on this south bank trail, for the valley was flat for a distance of half a mile away from the river, until the wooded uplands came down to join the plain. It meant retreating at a gallop ahead of the Indians, turning at intervals to pour lead into them and check their headlong pursuit. They lost several men in this retreat, for at that pace the going was treacherous for their horses, and many were thrown from their mounts and hacked down by the Indians before help could turn and go back to them.

They were still fighting desperately two hours later,

when unexpectedly they found a line of defences erected
at a point where the valley narrowed through a defile.
Two wagons had broken down on a steep gradient and
been abandoned by their owners, and these had been
drawn up across the trail, forming effective cover and a
tolerable barrier to the advance of the red men.

Afterwards they learned that these men of the wagons
– about fifteen of them – had ridden out from a small
town called Ephraim when the first of the fleeing wagon
loads of refugees drove into it. With good sense they had
seen the possibilities of the defile and had thrown up
defence works.

An hour later, however, the whole party was on the
retreat again. The defile had nearly become their death
trap.

With astonishing swiftness some agile Indians had
scaled an almost sheer bluff face and descended to the
valley behind them. It had taken the white men all their
time to fight their way through, but in the end they had
succeeded, and because their opponents were without
horses they were able to get a good start before the main
mass of Indians came pouring through the defile.

All that day they fought a running battle in the torrid
heat of the sun, sometimes holding up in suitable places
and giving their jaded mounts time to recover their wind,
other times riding for miles without pause.

Soon they began to come upon laggards from the
wagon-train, people whose vehicles had broken down or
whose horses could no longer pull their weight. In all
cases women and children had been taken off by other
wagoners, but in some of them were old and sick men who
had elected to stay behind rather than overburden
already tired horses.

These were picked up and ridden straight through to
Ephraim, where other wagons were setting off out of the
town. Like Massacre, the citizens of Ephraim had also
decided to abandon the place, and now the able-bodied men
rode out to join the hard-pressed settlers along the trail.

It gave new heart to them, to see these vigorous new allies, and when they came up the men from Massacre turned and struck back at their savage pursuers. But though their strength had been doubled by the reinforcements, they still had only seventy men to face several hundred.

The shock of that unexpected charge sent the red men careering away, but almost immediately the retreat began again as Indian columns were spotted far south of their position, attempting an encircling movement.

Shortly before sunset the weary cavalcade dropped down into the almost deserted town of Ephraim. All who were unable to fire a gun in defence of the place had been transported out on a wagon-train that was as long as the one that had left Massacre. By now the trail for fifty miles east must be almost solid with moving vehicles.

The Indians didn't attack before nightfall. All around Ephraim were many farms and smallholdings, and the wildly excited red men spent their time raiding these in preference to attacking a well-defended little town, stragetically situated in an ox-bow bend on the river.

Bose came round to tell them that they would rest up for the night in the town; they would hold on if they were attacked until nearly dawn, but they must slip away before daylight so that their force could still act as a barrier to the Indians along the river trail.

Andy Coan came and settled his aching old body alongside his friend. Their faces were grimed where the powder from their guns had exploded near their faces and covered them with a black deposit. He wasn't looking forward to another day in the saddle.

'How long c'n we keep this up, Joe?' he asked tiredly.

Cheyenne shrugged. 'I don't know. All I know is we've got to keep it up until them wagons get to safety.'

'That might take three or four more days.'

'Sure. I don't reckon the fastest wagons'll make it in less than three days from here, Andy. An' the slowest won't see Fort Tamberlin for five days or more.'

71

Andy lay back against the wall of a house, his eyes almost closed. 'We can't last out long, Joe. There's too many of the varmints. Why, ef they only used their guns now an' made a determined effort to cut the trail ahead of us, there's none of us would get through alive.'

Cheyenne watched westwards, to where the setting sun cast a blood-red light over the hills. Smoke was rising from a dozen points, and occasionally they saw flames as some unusually big fire added to the redness of the evening sky.

It was not a sight to cheer them.

Cheyenne said: 'That's not the way Injuns fight, Andy. Individually they're great, but they haven't the first idea of plannin' battles.' That was because war leaders, like White Fox, were invariably men jealous for battle honours and would take no part in anything that was not dramatic and spectacular and worth boasting about at the Scalp Dances around the ceremonial fires.

A guard was posted around the town for the night, while the rest saw to their horses and fed themselves, and then lay down anywhere in the deserted town to find sleep.

And no attack came during the hours of darkness. Doubtless the Indians were as fatigued from the day as they were.

They returned to wakefulness reluctantly when the guard came shaking them an hour before dawn. Almost it seemed as though they had never slept at all, and their bodies were just so many stiff, aching muscles that screamed in protest when they were made to move.

To Andy Coan and some of the other townspeople, no longer used to the saddle, it must have been sheer torture, yet gallantly they staggered to their feet and made no protest beyond an occasional groan.

Coffee was ready for them, thick, sweat, and strong. It seemed to do them more good than their hours of sleep, and it brought a cheerfulness to them and seemed to drive away the chill morning air.

72

Cheyenne helped Andy to get on to his horse. Bill Phelan had found a riderless mount back along the trail and was on his own now. Andy thought wistfully back to the triumph at Massacre town, and said: 'Ef I could find some powder I'd sure stay behind an' blow up more red varmints!'

But Bose wanted them to leave Ephraim by stealth, so as to get the Indians guessing, and he said there would be no gunpowder traps this time.

They rode silently out down the river trail, leaving an empty town back behind them in the blackness before dawn. As they rode they kept an alert watch, expecting some Indians to have gone ahead and lain in ambush, but they were not troubled.

That was just like Indians, to have an enemy at their mercy and yet to go riding off after easy plunder and throw away their chances of victory.

When dawn came they were many miles downstream, again in country suitable for defence. Now for many miles the river poured through a winding, narrow, tree-clad gorge. The Indians had lost their opportunity to encircle them, for they could not ride their horses through those trees at speed. And defence was easy, with a concentrated front and plenty of solid cover from which to fire.

The Indians, all the same, came pressing hard after them all that day. Clearly they were determined to break through to the rich lands of the Missouri basin, and this gorge offered the quickest way out for them.

At first they tried their usual tactics of storming up on their wild little ponies, but seventy rifles, shooting from behind tree trunks, beat back every wave of attackers. In time the Indians learned sense, and then they left their horses and began a steady infiltration through the trees. When they did that the defenders lost their advantage, for now the cover was as good for the Indians as it was for themselves.

All the same, the Indians could only make slow progress on foot, and that satisfied the white men. This rearguard action of theirs must be invaluable to the slow wagons fleeing just ahead of them. Perhaps after all they might find the safety that the defenders were fighting for.

Hour by hour the white men retreated along that wooded gorge. They lost twenty men in a distance of seven miles, but they gained the better part of a day for the women and children and they thought it was worth while.

That night they were attacked by a horde of Indians who were no longer cock-a-whoop and exhilarated with thoughts of easy victory – now they were vicious and sullen and determined to wipe out the hard-pressed band of men who fought so tenaciously against overwhelming odds. Now, perhaps, their leaders regretted the wasted opportunities of the day before, when they had had them in much easier country. But an Indian was always side-tracked by loot.

The attack was beaten off, but Greg Bose thought it better to pull his main force back a few miles so as not to get surrounded in the dark. It proved a fortunate move, for the Indians tried to sneak round them, over the hill tops, in the darkness, only when they came down on to the trail again it was to find that they were still in front of the enemy and not in their rear as they had supposed.

When dawn came the settlers had less than fifty men, and the gorge seemed choked with Indians intent on sweeping out into the open country beyond. And that retreat in the night had brought Bose and his party to within a few hundred yards of the end of the gorge.

Bose rode among them shortly after daybreak.

'Ef these Injuns drive us out on to the plain,' he told them, 'we'll all be dead within ten minutes. Them critters has got their backs up, and they sure intend to wipe us out ef it's the last thing they can do.

'So we don't let 'em drive us out.' he said bluntly. 'We hang on to this gorge an' keep 'em bottled up as long as possible. We stay here an' die here, if necessary, but we don't pull out from this valley.'

He spoke sense. But Greg Bose always spoke sense.

74

Better to die here, holding back the Indian horde, than to die out on the plain and let their enemies race unchecked after their womenfolk.

The Indians seemed to divine their object, and in eagerness to be through to the rich hunting grounds now less than a mile from them, they flung themselves into the attack with reckless abandon.

From the first it became apparent that the position was hopeless, that with men dying steadily it was only a question of time before the enemy was through. But resolutely the settlers fought on, fought till their fingers were blistered by the heat of their guns, fought until they were nearly deaf from the barking of their rifle. Fought, though no man there thought they had a chance of survival.

Two hours later the biggest attack of all suddenly developed. Cheyenne, down among some rocks only a few yards from the rushing river, saw hundreds of near-naked brown bodies begin a relentless march through the trees above them. This time by sheer weight the Indians intended to smash their way through – and now not many more than thirty rifles spoke against them.

It seemed that within minutes they would be overrun, when suddenly there was a roar like thunder that seemed to start behind them and then travel up that winding gorge like an invisible train. It was followed by a whistling sound, as of a mighty wind, and then a tree was smashed in half and the great leafy top came somersaulting down among the other trees until it settled right across the trail they had fought so long to guard.

Cheyenne saw Andy Coan's startled face, looked into eyes that were as incredulous as his own. Then both whipped round.

Two field guns had been deployed a hundred yards back of them. The gunners were crouching round them. As they watched the second of the guns puffed white smoke, and then another cannon ball whizzed past them and created havoc in the trees where the astonished Indians were.

A dozen cavalry, their work of escorting the field guns at an end, came riding up to support the defenders. Sight of the blue-uniformed reinforcements brought the defenders on to their feet. In a moment a great, ringing cheer went echoing along the valley. The way they shouted, anyone would have thought that a couple of hundred cavalry had arrived, and perhaps that was how the Indians imagined it. They couldn't see round the bend; all they knew was that cannon had arrived and that meant that the dreaded United States army with their fine weapons were there.

The Indians stopped their attack, though had they known it they could have swept the defences away without any great bother, and by the time they realized that the reinforcements were light their opportunity to hurt had gone for ever.

For reinforcements came rushing up to help the settlers. East of those hills people realized that if the Indian horde poured out on to the Missouri plains they would create tremendous havoc, therefore every attempt must be made to hold them back now. So they came in from all the surrounding area, settler after settler racing up with his much-needed rifle. And by nightfall over two hundred men, apart from the handful of soldiers, were guarding the passage to the great eastern plains.

The men from Massacre and Ephraim had won out. They had bought time to save their people – time expensive in life and limb. But at least the women and children were safe now.

They were weary men when they were relieved by newcomers and went tiredly across to where camp-fires were burning and there was food cooking and plenty of good hot coffee. Too tired to receive the congratulations of the newcomers, whose land they had saved from invasion.

But not too tired to receive visitors. At least Cheyenne found that someone was expecting to speak with him before he slept.

It was the bearded lieutenant in charge of the soldiers.

He sought Cheyenne out and shook his hand warmly. 'Your letter came through to Fort Tamberlin in time,' he said. 'The commanding officer sent us immediately to give what help we could.'

Cheyenne smiled. 'He didn't send many.'

'No.' The lieutenant shook his head. 'But he hasn't many troops at his disposal just now. I'm afraid this war will have to be fought by settlers and not by the army, for it'll take a week at least before they can move up troops from the east.'

'Then,' said Cheyenne, 'it will be a bloody, savage war.' For settlers would fight viciously, because of the injury they had suffered; they would give no quarter to any Indian they met.

And then the lieutenant handed a telegram to Cheyenne. The Indian agent read it. It was from Washington. It said: 'ORDER YOU APPROACH WARRING CHIEFS WITHOUT DELAY AND OFFER PEACE TERMS.'

CHAPTER SIX

GALBRAY!

Cheyenne sighed and handed the telegram to Andy Coan to read. Andy exploded. 'The fools!' he exclaimed wrathfully. 'Do they think you c'n ride up to an Injun holdin' a scalpin' knife in his hand an' start talkin' peace?'

And Cheyenne had no illusions, either. There was no possible chance of success if he did ride out to meet the Indians. The Cheyennes especially would think that he had tricked them and they would be cruelly vindictive.

Cheyenne tossed the telegram into the fire. That was all it was good for – fuel for the leaping flames. Then he went and slept, and not all the gunfire along that echoing valley disturbed him until morning.

Next day a long column of men came riding in from the east, doubling their strength. Cheyenne and Andy Coan stood by the trail side and watched them come in. They were the roughest bunch of border ruffians that Cheyenne had ever seen. Good fighting men, but crude and brutal in their strength.

They learned that these were a hastily recruited regiment of volunteers from townships in Kansas, in which territory they now were. They called themselves the Hundred Day Volunteers, having bound themselves to serve for that period before disbandment.

Andy spoke softly, watching the horsemen ride steadily

past in a cloud of yellow dust. 'God help the Injuns if these fellars get hold of 'em!'

Cheyenne nodded bitterly. 'Yes. These are as much savages as White Fox and his Strong Hearts.' Always these loungers and wastrels from around the towns were the most bloodthirsty of soldiers; but then they volunteered almost as much for the chance of killing as for the plunder they would get in any disturbance.

Then Cheyenne stiffened. He had seen a familiar face. Then he saw another – and another. The men who had tortured that Indian staked out by the fire that night were riding with these Kansas Volunteers. He thought they must have taken alarm at his escape and had ridden out of the country; now emboldened by the general upheaval following the Indian uprising, they were venturing back in the hope of rich spoils. Often men came out wealthy from wars like these . . .

The men from Massacre and Ephraim townships were ordered east by the lieutenant with the dead and wounded. They had done their share of fighting and were exhausted and needed rest, he told them. They were not sorry for a chance to recover from their ordeal, and with all these white men blasting the Indians back out of the gulch there was no need for them any longer.

Cheyenne rode with them, but it was to send a telegram off to the Indian Office in Washington. It was short, even terse, and the eye-shaded telegraphist lifted his eyes in appreciation when it was handed to him. It said, 'That was the silliest order I have ever received – stop – Accept my resignation – stop – Joe Shay.'

He was through with the Indian Office. They were a set of bunglers who thought they could watch over the red man's interests from the comforts of Washington, more than a thousand miles away.

When he came out of the telegraph office he felt better. Then he saw a sight that turned him sour again.

He saw a detachment of cavalry come jigging down the dusty street of this small town on the telegraph line out

79

to Fort Kearney. And among the reinforcements was – Captain Jules Galbray.

Cheyenne jumped for his own horse and wheeled out after the soldiers, but they came to a halt outside an army depot only a few yards further down the street. Cheyenne pushed his mount through the cavalry until he came to Galbray's side. He tapped him on the shoulder.

Galbray turned, and his brown eyes went wide as if from shock. Cheyenne felt his pulse racing. Galbray clearly hadn't been pleased to see him.

He said, 'I'd like a word with you, Captain.'

Galbray hesitated and glanced quickly towards his men, as if seeking an excuse for delay among them. Then he shrugged. He was a bold man, as befitted one of the hard-riding American cavalry.

'OK,' he assented. 'What do you want to know?' He made no effort to dismount.

Most of the men had hitched to a rail by now and gone inside where it was cool and shady. Only one man was fiddling about under his saddle, as if padding a sore on his mount's back.

Cheyenne spoke levelly. 'Maybe you c'n guess what I want to know, Captain. What happened to Commissioner Wade Pengelly – an' one hundred thousand dollars in bounty?'

Galbray spoke, and now he never batted an eyelid. 'We got attacked by Injuns. The wagon was burnt out an' we had to skedaddle in quick time to keep our hides intact.'

'Attacked? Out on the flats?' Cheyenne's voice was ironical.

'Nope.' Captain Galbray spoke with cold assurance. 'We was attacked out on the trail to Cheyenne territory.'

'It was agreed you should stay near to Massacre till I sent word it was safe for you to come into the agency.'

'After you'd gone, the commissioner changed his mind. He opined it was better to get that money into the Injuns' hands an' so keep 'em quiet. He was worried because of the outbreak up in Luther country.'

It was glib. Cheyenne knew there was more to it than that, knew there was a lie on this lean-faced captain's lips. But suspecting is one thing; being able to nail a lie another. He had to appear to accept the story.

'We went out with the immigrants to have company for the first ten miles or so of the way. Then we parted with them, and struck south-west to where the Cheyennes were known to be in camp.' Galbray gave out the further details without prompting, and to Cheyenne it sounded like a man who was repeating a well-rehearsed story.

'The man's too glib,' he thought. Aloud he said, 'An' then you were attacked?'

'Yeah. Suddenly there was Injuns everywhere. We saw there was no chance, so we rode away hell-for-leather, leavin' the wagon to the varmints.'

'You said they burnt your wagon?'

Galbray had an answer for that. 'We didn't ride so fast we couldn't look behind us.' He spoke toughly, challengingly now. He was so sure of the strength of his story that he felt able to defend himself by going over to the attack.

'We saw smoke risin' after we'd ridden away. We guessed it was the wagon goin' up in flames.'

Cheyenne spoke thoughtfully. 'That's queer. Injuns don't burn things that are useful to them. If you'd run away, why did they go an' burn the wagon?'

Captain Galbray froze in his saddle, and his voice came out harshly. 'You callin' me a liar, Shay?'

'I'm tellin' you I don't think much to your story,' retorted Cheyenne. 'It was too convenient, a fire which destroyed a hundred thousand dollars.' Only when he came to the word destroyed he lent sarcasm to it, and there was no disguising his meaning.

Captain Galbray suddenly retreated. He swung out of the saddle, saying gruffly, 'You find Commissioner Pengelly an' tell him what you think. I'm a soldier. I obey orders. I did all I could to protect that wagon, an' if you think different you'll find yourself in trouble.'

Then he went quickly within the depot. His final words

were tough and threatening, but all the same he spoke them on the retreat. Cheyenne thought, grimly, 'I made him uneasy. He didn't want to keep talkin' to me.' And he wondered how much the treacherous cavalry captain had received of the hundred thousand dollars – and what he had done with it.

He rode away down to where he had found lodgings along with Andy Coan and some of the Massacre men. It was in an upstairs back room run by a woman who had been widowed in an earlier Indian uprising, and she was making quite a fuss of them.

He stabled his horse across the road, then slowly crossed the sun-bright street and found the welcome shade within the apartment house. He let the door swing to behind him, crossed the small hall and began to mount the creaking wooden steps. He went slowly; he was a very dispirited man.

And then he heard the door open below him, heard it slam to. Heard feet cross the hall and begin to mount the step just behind him. And they were hurrying as if to overtake him.

And suddenly the thought came to him that this might spell danger – suddenly he turned and sat back on the stairs, and as he turned his Colt came leaping into his hand.

A blue-uniformed soldier stopped short, looking into that ugly muzzle. Cheyenne thought, 'I've seen you before,' and then decided it was the fellow who had been so long attending to the sores on his horse's back.

He asked, ironically, 'You fixed them sores on your hoss' back, brother?'

The soldier never took his eyes away from that gun. It seemed to hold for him the fascination of a snake for a rabbit. Yet his voice was quite even when he replied, 'It didn't have no sores, mister. My hosses don't ever get sores, 'cause I guess I like hoss-flesh.'

Then he lifted his eyes. Cheyenne saw that the trooper was only a kid, and those blue eyes were as straight and honest as any he had ever seen.

The trooper seemed to be able to read his thoughts, for

he said, still quietly, 'You can put that cannon away, mister. I didn't come here to do you harm.'

Cheyenne shoved the Colt back in his holster, trusting him. But he didn't move up the stairs – this place was as good as any to hear the fellar's business. The trooper sighed and sat down on the widow's threadbare stairs carpet.

'You don't trust me. Wal, I reckon I don't blame you,' said the kid. 'These days nobody can trust anybody, can they?'

'I don't trust Galbray.' Cheyenne said it deliberately. He had realized that this trooper might be able to give him valuable information, and he wanted to encourage the boy to speak.

'You'd be a fool if you did. He's twister than a corkscrew that's been married to a spiral staircase, that fellar.'

'Were you in the party that was detailed to guard the commissioner and that bounty?'

The trooper nodded. 'That's why I followed you. I heard you askin' questions of Galbray, an' I heard some of his replies.'

'And Galbray,' Chayenne prompted softly, 'was lying?'

The trooper's answer came as a surprise. 'Nope. So far as I know, what he said was the truth.'

Cheyenne felt disappointed, and then his quick mind seized upon five words 'So far as you know.'

The trooper started to talk, then. 'Mighty queer things happened after we got half a day into Cheyenne territory.' Joe Shay thought quickly. Half a day . . . they'd be a long way from the big Cheyenne camping ground, where the tribe was congregating. From the numbers there, he didn't think there could be many braves out on the war trails.

'After we'd been rollin' a time, Cap'n Galbray went up to a hill. He came down almost at once an' said there was Injuns on our trail, an' he told off a sergeant an' all but two of the men to go back down the trail an' head 'em off. The cap'n went on with the commissioner, the commissioner's teamster – an' two troopers.'

He paused. Cheyenne thought, 'He wants to say some-thin' about them troopers.' So he asked, 'What kinda fellars was them troopers like, friend?'

The boy answered. 'Ef I wasn't in someone's house, I reckon I'd spit.'

'Like that, huh?'

'Worse. A couple of thievin', scroungin' no-goods, who were a disgrace to the regiment. But Galbray deliberately picked 'em to go up with him.' His finger idly traced patterns on the faded wallpaper. 'I reckoned at the time that was a bit queer.'

'What happened after that?'

'We rode back along the trail, but there wasn't a sight of any Injuns. Then we heard firin' along where the wagon had gone, an' we turned to see what was happenin'. A few minutes later Cap'n Galbray, the commissioner an' the others came ridin' back along the trail.'

'All of 'em?'

'All of 'em.'

Cheyenne looked thoughtfully at a picture of the land-lady's bearded father, but it gave him no inspiration. All he could think was that it was a queer fight with Indians where no one got killed.

'What did Galbray say?'

'He shouted that the Injuns must have given us the slip an' come ridin' round 'em, an' it was no good tryin' to take 'em all on. He ordered us all to ride hell-for-leather for Rock Ridge on the Republican River. Which we did. We saw the smoke of that wagon an' we didn't stop to argue. It was only when we reached Rock Ridge that I began to think.'

He was an intelligent boy, this trooper, destined to become a crack cavalry officer himself, one day.

'And what did you think?'

'I thought it was queer that Injuns on the warpath didn't come ridin' after us. If there had been hundreds attackin' that wagon, I'd have said for certain they'd have high-tailed after our scalps. But we never saw an Injun, not from start to finish.'

'Except Captain Galbray.'

'Except the cap'n.'

They sat in silence for a while, then Cheyenne asked, 'When they came ridin' back along the trail, were they carryin' anythin' – the commissioner, Galbray, an' the others?'

The trooper considered. 'Nope,' he said, after a while. 'Not that I could see. You're thinkin' about them dollar bills?' He was shrewd.

Cheyenne nodded.

'They didn't bring them with them,' the boy said with certainty. 'Not all of them. That treasury chest was pretty big, an I reckon a hundred thousand dollars must weigh close on three hundredweight. Maybe they helped themselves to a few handfuls, as much as they could stuff into their pockets without causin' suspicion. Yeah, I reckon they would do that, help themselves to some of the dough. Them fellars wasn't the kind to leave good money lyin' around. But all the same, they didn't bring all that money with them.'

'It's queer.' Cheyenne stood up now. This didn't make sense to him. 'They each take a handful of dollar bills an' burn the rest. It don't add up.'

And it didn't.

He said to the trooper, 'Reckon I owe you some thanks for comin' an' talkin' to me, friend. Sorry I kinda acted quick with my gun when you came in after me.'

The boy said drily, 'So that's what you call it? The way it came out looked quicker than quick to me.'

Cheyenne laughed. 'What's your name? Mine's Joe Shay, Indian agent – resigned.'

'I know you.' The trooper nodded. 'That's why I came to you. Everyone tells me you're on the level, else I might have thought you were mixed up in this.' He said he was named Cole Newark.

Cheyenne told him he would be riding west again, into the fighting. Cole Newark looked at him levelly, then said, 'You aim to catch up with the commissioner an' Galbray.' He didn't invite a comment on his remark, being sure of what he said. 'Wal, I'd watch out ef I was you, mister. That Pengelly's smile takes everyone in at first, but he sure is pisen.'

Then he went. Cheyenne walked up to his room, found fat Andy Coan resting on his bed, and told him about his visitor. When he had finished he said, 'I'm goin' back, Andy. A lot of people are gettin' hurt because of mean redskins like White Fox an' meaner white men like Pengelly. I intend to make both answer for their crimes.'

And Andy Coan said almost the same words as the trooper. 'Watch your step, Joe. Ef them varmints know you're trailin' 'em, they'll turn on you an' kill you out of hand.' He added after a brief pause, 'They'd be fools not to, either, with you aimin' to get 'em all strung up for causin' this war.'

Back across the dusty plain rode the tall young frontiersman. He felt better now than he had done since the Indian girl had stabbed him with his own Bowie.

The lingering stiffness in the muscle of his left arm was a constant reminder of the girl, and he found himself thinking a great deal of her. He wondered where she was and what she was doing. Indian fashion, he guessed that she and the womenfolk of the tribe wouldn't be far behind their warriors. He found himself praying that no sudden rush of white men should break through and cut off the Cheyenne folk, for he dreaded to think what would happen to the girl if she fell into the hands of border cutthroats like those eager Hundred Day Volunteers from Kansas.

Always, he began to notice, when he thought of the possible peril of the Indian maiden, he found himself unconsciously urging his horse into a faster pace. And then in time, he became honest with himself. In time he began to realize that he wasn't only going back west to bring justice to erring reds and whites. He was going back to try to find the Indian girl and save her from horrors that would most likely end in death.

If he could bring the miscreants of both peoples to book, he wouldn't waste any opportunity. But he realized that such activities would be incidental beside the main purpose of his return.

The fighting had moved through the wooded gorge when he reached it and was erupting on to the flat lands beyond. As he rode between the precipitous, tree-clothed hill, he saw scenes of devastation all the way along the narrow valley.

Those clumsy field guns, of greater use in scaring wild Indian ponies than in the damage they could wreak, had uprooted trees where solid iron balls had impacted against them. All in among the vegetation were bodies. Some were white, and many were without scalps but the majority were red and bare save for a breech clout – and vengeful white men had scalped these in turn.

Some men found pleasure in such sights, Cheyenne knew, but it sickened him. So he rode on quickly, though the trees gave a welcome shade against the great heat, and it was cool and pleasant to ride so close to the rushing, mountain torrent.

As he came to the far end of the gorge, where their desperate rearguard battle with the Indians had really begun, he heard the sound of gunfire and the occasional boom of a big gun.

He rode out into the open, on to the heels of the soldiers and Hundred Day Volunteers. The Indians were streaming out across the plains in retreat, but the officer commanding the whites, an infantry major, ordered that no pursuit of them should be made yet. He was wise enough to know that if he allowed his force to split up after the Indians, their value would be considerably reduced. The Indians were still in far greater numbers, and would annihilate small parties that were foolish enough to be enticed into pursuit.

The officer left a strong force to guard the key pass through the range, and then marched on to Ephraim, where he intended to set up headquarters.

Nobody expected to find much left of the town, so everyone was surprised to see that no damage had been done to it by marauding Indians. Cheyenne made a guess – once bitten, twice shy, the Indians had skirted the town thinking this might be another trap like Massacre. They weren't inclined to go into any town which might blow up under their feet the moment they got there.

It was nightfall when the troops rode into Ephraim, and then followed scenes that beggared description. The saloons had been left with full bottles on the shelves and beer in the barrels in the cellars. When the men realized this, they stormed into the saloons and fought to get their hands on the free liquor. Within half an hour the town was filled with drink-crazed men who roamed through the streets and picked quarrels with each other and did almost as much damage to themselves with their gun play as the Indians had inflicted in the last hours of fighting.

The major saw the danger and marched all the troops away from the centre of the town. If the Indians attacked, there must be some sober enough to drive them off, he told his men.

But the Indians didn't attack that night. The Indians had had a licking and they were now roaming the plains in search of victories easier than tackling a well-armed regiment of trained soldiers and volunteers. They had lost their war already, just as Cheyenne had prophesied. War paint wasn't any good any longer, not against Winchesters.

Next day the situation was still out of hand. The Hundred Day Volunteers awoke sore and not a little drunk, and immediately went back for more liquor. Drunkenness was bad enough at night-time, but when the hot sun poured upon them it drove the fumes to their brains and sent them crazy.

The commanding officer had wanted to send strong bodies of men riding out to drive the marauding bands of Indians back into their territory, but with more than half his force hopelessly drunk he was obliged to sit around the town for another full day and curse the insobriety of his followers.

In the evening, after the lamps were lit, the uproar

seemed to reach new heights. Bad-tempered, sore-headed men picked quarrels too easily, and there was fighting in the streets and gun-play in the saloons.

Cheyenne got out of the way of it all and retired to sleep in a hay-loft above the livery stable where he had found a place for his horse.

An hour later some men came to kill him.

They were four of the men who had raided Sycamore Creek and tortured Blue Flower's father. They must have spotted Cheyenne's return to the town and had lain in wait for him. They were stone-cold sober, though they pretended to be drunk, and clearly they hoped to dispose of their enemy in the general confusion in the town. People weren't going to comment over any individual body with all that killing going on in the town.

Cheyenne heard them as they entered the stable below. They had kept out of his sight while he was in Ephraim, but he had guessed they were around and he had anticipated trouble from them sometime. So when they started to fire up at the ceiling, as drunken men might do in their hilarity, he was ready for it and simply jumped out from the loft window into the sandy back lane.

Someone spotted his escape from the yard door and shouted, and then three other men ran out into the moonlight and began to fire recklessly. Cheyenne had his Colt out and triggered three times, but the range was rather great and he didn't hope to do much damage.

Two of the men had brought rifles, and as soon as he heard the high-powered bullets screech past his ear, Cheyenne started to duck backwards down the narrow alleys between the crazy leaning buildings. The men showed they weren't drunk by displaying quite a lot of sagacity in trying to get ahead of him to cut him off. Once he nearly got caught, as one of his opponents almost dropped on to him from the roof of a low, connecting building, but Cheyenne wheeled in time and sent a bullet at the man. It didn't kill him, but the way the man swore he didn't seem to like where it had gone, either.

Then Cheyenne got out into the main street, where so many people were staggering and brawling about that another fight made no difference. He saw his opponents deliberately walk down the street after him. They had determined to kill him this night, and weren't going to be stopped by the openness of their position.

Cheyenne, armed only with his Colt, could only keep moving backwards, taking cover all the time against the possibility of a rifle shot. He suddenly realized how alone he was in this town, now that all his Massacre friends were recovering from their injuries in distant Kansas.

Then he came alongside a hide merchant's office, saw the yellow, gleaming light of lamps within, and remembered that this was the office of the commanding officer of the United States forces.

He marched inside. He would denounce the four men as desperadoes who had in part caused this vicious war.

Captain Jules Galbray lifted his thin, high cheekboned face to greet him.

Cheyenne said, 'I want to speak to the major.' He stood with his back to the wall, watching the open doorway. Outside in the darkness were four desperate men waiting for him. He realized that Galbray was alone in the office.

Galbray said, shortly, 'He's campin' out of town with his men. Anythin' I c'n do for you?'

Cheyenne wasn't sure. He caught a stir out beyond the pool of yellow light that made the board sidewalk a pattern of long shadows. It decided him. There was death outside. Galbray's duty was to help him. All right, he would tell the captain of those desperadoes and would see what Galbray did about it.

He said, 'There's four men outside gunnin' for me, cap'n.'

Galbray put down a quill pen and said, 'Have they got good reason, Shay?' and his voice was completely colourless and unemotional.

'Yeah.' Cheyenne nodded. 'You could say they have. They were in the party that committed the massacre along Sycamore Creek an' helped to cause all this rumpus. I caught them torturin' an Injun, an' they want to kill me because they know I'll hand 'em over to authority when I catch 'em, an' they'll maybe get hung.'

'So they don't intend to let you catch them?' Cheyenne looked at those dark brown eyes set in that face that was so thin it looked as though brown paper only had been stretched over the skull bones. He was trying to read the thoughts in this man's mind, but it was almost impossible again.

He nodded. 'Reckon that's about it. Give me some men an' let me go after 'em. Now I know they're in town I'm determined to bring 'em to face justice.'

Galbray said nothing.

Cheyenne said, 'Why don't you send for some men, captain?'

Galbray looked at his quill pen. 'Because,' he said deliberately, 'you're drunk, Shay, and I don't hand over soldiers for a drunken man to use as he thinks fit.'

For a second that statement rocked Cheyenne, and then he understood and recovered. Galbray wasn't calling him drunk just to annoy him; he was saying what he intended to say if there were any questions afterwards. 'I didn't believe Shay. The man seemed drunk when he came to me.' That was as good an alibi as anything, with a town full of uproariously drunken men.

And if he had had any doubts before about the soldier, now Cheyenne had none. This man was his enemy. This man would seek his death no less bitterly than those four desperadoes out in the street.

Cheyenne crouched, his eyes blazing. 'You mean—'

Gilbray said brusquely, 'I mean, Shay, get out of this office! Go on, beat it!'

And there was a gun in his hand, a big Navy Colt that looked like a cannon. All the time it had lain under the hat that was on the table ready for an emergency such as this.

Cheyenne looked at him, his head slowly nodding. This Galbray man was smart. He was going to drive him out into the street to meet his death at the hands of those other desperadoes lurking in the shadows. It was all very convenient.

He drawled, playing for time, 'Pity you haven't them two troopers with you. Galbray.'

Galbray bit. 'What troopers?'

'The pair that could be expected to keep their mouths shut if they were given a fistful of dollar bills.' His eyes never left Galbray's dark face. He thought that his stab went home, but couldn't be sure, so he tried again.

His voice was softer. 'Such a pair would kill a man if they were told to, I reckon.' Galbray's eyes were hard on his own, and now they seemed as bright and black as a rattlesnake's. 'An old man, anyway. A man with an old gun an' a voice that could only come from Kentucky an' a coonskin cap to match.'

Galbray never batted an eyelid. He just pointed the revolver and said, 'I don't want to kill you, Shay, but I'll do it if you keep talkin'. March out through those doors an' keep your hands up all the time or I'll kill you.'

Cheyenne saw something move above the sill of an open window. He began to open his mouth in instinctive warning, and then he thought, 'It can't make my position worse.'

He hadn't done himself much good by trying to report matters to the commanding officer.

He turned, hands lifted. The lamp threw his shadow across the floor and half-way up a side wall. If he moved towards the door his shadow would move with him, he mused. And the moment his shadow was full across the board sidewalk, some hidden marksman across the street would sight a gun and blow his head off.

He decided he wanted to keep his head where it was, but he couldn't quite see how to do it.

Then the question was settled for him. A gun bumped off, setting the hanging oil lamp to dancing. He saw a heavy, Navy Colt jump into the air and then hit the end of the table before falling on to the floor – saw an astonished

92

army officer clutch his right hand under his left arm as if it were stunned.

Then Galbray started to go down after the Colt, and this time there was murder in his eyes.

CHAPTER SEVEN

WANTED -
PROOF!

Cheyenne could have killed him. As it was he came out
with his revolver even before that Colt had hit the table.
But if he had killed an army officer while on active service
in the field, regardless of any defence he might put up, he
would become an outlaw in the sight of justice. And
Cheyenne didn't want to be branded an outlaw and live
out his life on the owlhoot trails.

He jumped towards the window, through which had
come that fortunate shot. He didn't know who could have
come to his rescue in so timely a fashion, and right then
he didn't have time to think about, it.

He jumped straight through the open window, risking
a broken leg in the darkness beyond. Someone was
running swiftly down the back alley, dodging among the
straggling, unplanned buildings that lined it.

Cheyenne set his long legs into pursuit – but he was
also seeking to put as great a distance as possible
between himself and the four desperadoes. It was too one-
sided, taking on four killers after dark in a town like this.

He never caught that man ahead of him. The fellow
was as lithe as a greyhound and nearly as fast. In less

than half a minute Cheyenne had lost his trail.

He paused back of a noisy saloon. There seemed to be a meeting of some kind being held there, for at times there was silence, followed by a great roaring cheer. The men had grown tired of drinking – or perhaps the liquor had run out – and now they seemed intent on some other fun.

Cheyenne debated his next move. He didn't dare risk a return for his horse, because he was sure by now at least one of his enemies would be waiting in ambush for his return. And without a horse he couldn't leave this town, hostile though it was to him.

On an impulse he walked round and into the saloon. If he mixed with the thick crowd within he stood a chance of escaping detection by his pursuers. Besides, he was intrigued to know what was happening at this unexpected meeting in the big saloon.

He pushed his way through the throng near to the crowded doorway. It was stiflingly hot inside, so that the sweat broke out on his face immediately, and within seconds his shirt was sticking to his back. The fumes of rank tobacco assailed him, biting into his eyes and burning his lungs.

It took him seconds to focus through the haze above the heads of the men, but at last he began to make out the scene. A staircase led out from one corner of the saloon, giving access to the top floor. At a bend in the staircase a small group of men was standing, gripping the rail and looking down upon the bleary-eyed audience below.

A man was speaking. Cheyenne heard the man's words before he saw his face. A rich, vibrant voice shouted, 'The only good Injun's a dead 'un!' And at that there was a roar of approval from the throng below.

The speaker went on, 'These Injuns break out an' slaughter every white man within hundreds of miles, an' what does the commandin' officer say? He says, "Drive 'em back into their territory an' hold 'em there." That's all he says. Just drive 'em back to where they started from!'

Cheyenne was trying to get his head round a tall man's tall hat so as to be able to see the speaker, but for a few seconds he wasn't being successful. There was something about that voice that intrigued him—

'Are we goin' to stand for such kidglove methods?' the speaker demanded.

'No,' came back a mighty roar from the befuddled crowd.

'I say let's teach 'em a lesson for all time, these murderin' Injuns!' Cheyenne was getting his head round the obstruction now. 'I say, to hell with the army an' their instructions from Washington – let's ride in after them Injuns, into their reservation, an' let's take the scalps of the lot of 'em. A dead Injun won't ever do a white man any harm. Let's kill the lot! Death to the red man wherever he is!'

Then the roof went off. It was a sentiment that seemed to appeal to every man there, and they stamped their feet in approval until the saloon shook and threatened to collapse in on them, and they roared agreement and took up the cry, 'Death to all Injuns.'

And then Cheyenne saw the speaker. It was smooth-voiced Wade Pengelly, Commissioner from Washington's Indian Office and paid representative of the red man's interests.

And Wade Pengelly was whipping up the fury of this besotted audience, demanding that they should go out and kill every red man they saw.

Cheyenne went berserk at the duplicity of the trickster. He had met many smooth-tongued twisters from back east before, but this man was the worst yet.

He fought his way through the throng, and when men resented the roughness of his passage and lashed out at him he turned and lashed back at them. And one way or another he got through and then went stamping up those steps behind Pengelly.

He had yet again an impression of mighty-thewn limbs, braced apart against that railing – again he got the impression of a man who seemed soft with his smooth voice and pink cheeks, but who wasn't soft at all, but had iron muscles and a brutal, callous will to match.

When he came up over the top step he didn't pause. If he were to secure the support of any section of this audience he had to employ bold methods, much as he had done back in Massacre against a bloodthirsty teamster.

So he crashed with all his weight against Pengelly, and the railing collapsed and all the men who were leaning on it fell in among the people below. Pengelly must have gone down harder than the others, for when he fell he stayed down on the floor, knocked unconscious by the fall.

The crowd gasped, then decided to be very interested. Action was what they craved for, and Cheyenne's arrival on those stairs was certainly dramatic.

He called for quietness. 'I want you to listen to me,' he shouted. 'This fellow you've been listening to is a no-good trickster from Washington. I don't know his game, but he's tryin' to use you for some plan of his own.'

A drunken voice roared out, 'We ain't bein' used for nothin'. That fellar was talkin' more sense than I've heard in the last ten years. Kill all red men, that's what I say, too!'

And at that another mighty shout of approval went up from the throng, and with it Cheyenne's hopes fell to zero. This crowd was determined on blood, and he guessed there was no way of changing their thoughts at this late hour.

But he tried. He shouted, 'There's half a million red men left in America. You can't slaughter them all.'

In their mood that audience could consider the slaughter of any number of red men, and they shouted him down. He kept on trying to speak, tried to make them see sense – tried to get them to understand that the slaughter of Indian women and children must lead to reprisals – white women and children in isolated places must suffer, too. Always that was the pattern of Indian warfare.

'Some day it's got to stop,' he shouted. 'Some day we'll

all live side by side in peace – an' there's enough for every-one in America, red and white alike.'

Then that drunk stood on a table and shouted: 'If we kill them red varmints, then there'll be all that more for us!' And again he got a roar of applause for his crude wit.

The crowd resented the ex-Indian agent's intervention. They wanted talk such as Pengelly had given them they didn't want talk which sounded near to preaching to their rough ears. And they began to press forward, their cries growing ugly and threatening. Cheyenne, for all his own hot anger, realized that he was in an unpleasant situation – he thought, 'All this night I seem to have been jumping from one darned shindig to another!'

Then a man began to shout: 'That's Cheyenne Joe, the Injun's agent. He's a damn' renegade, always stickin' up for the Injuns. Let's string him up!'

Renegade! There it went again. Always that word was hurled at him when people got their hackles up.

Renegade! If Andy Coan, Bill Phelan and some of the old timers from Massacre town had been there they could have told a different story. They knew that Cheyenne Joe was no traitor to his kind. Cheyenne had done too much for the white settlers all up the Smoky Hill River for them to misunderstand his strivings on behalf of the suspicious, always-dangerous red man. It was the newcomers – especially the vicious hangers-on who flocked to every frontier town – who read the worst in his actions and who slandered him.

If Commissioner Pengelly and a lot of other Indian agents had been as true to their duty as he, there would never have been any Indian riots and uprisings.

Four men were standing at the foot of the stairs, and one carried a rope on which was already fashioned a noose.

Four men, heads lowered to watch him from under shaggy eyebrows like so many savage Texas longhorns – but in their eyes was the sparkle of grim, sardonic humour – the four men who had tortured that Indian and had tried to shoot him down, here in this drink-crazy town.

This was much better, hanging him. They could shut his mouth without bringing danger to themselves, and they could have some sport with him at the same time.

Three guns covered him – two rifles and one revolver. If he tried to go for his own gun he would only be cheating them out of a hanging, for he would be killed before he could clear leather.

They started to come up those stairs, and behind them pressed the drink inflamed, blood-lusting Hundred Day Volunteers. The din was now of such heights that the crouching agent on the bend of the stairs couldn't have been heard if he had shouted at the top of his lungs.

Then somebody started to shoot out the swinging oil lamps.

The first ones to go were at the end of the room by the stairs. Cheyenne heard the shattering of glass, saw a wildly swinging brass lamp extinguish the yellow flame by the draught of its own movement. He threw himself down against the broad stairs that led upwards from the big saloon. A second lamp went out and he was left in deep shadow. Then the other two lamps exploded and the saloon was in complete darkness.

Cheyenne raced up the stairs like lightning, and only just in time for some of the men below, anticipating his line of retreat, brought up their guns and blazed away in the darkness in the general direction of those stairs.

Down below the saloon rocked as men fought to get out – their struggles brought reprisals and within seconds the whole place was a mass of brawling, furious men, striking out indiscriminately, yet not knowing quite why they did it.

It gave Cheyenne a chance to escape, and he took it. What was more, because he knew the throng would hold up those four pursuing killers, he could risk returning for his horse and ride out of town in search of pleasanter quarters.

He lowered himself on to a sloping roof at the back of the saloon, then dropped into a fenced yard in which were stored the empty barrels and crates. The fence proved no obstacle – in fact, because it demonstrated that his arm was no handicap to him now, it served to improve his confidence. He pulled himself up, sat on the fence and peered around in the pale moonlight, then dropped lightly into the alley below.

He had hoped to see again this intruder who came at such a fortuitous moment. Twice in one night he had rescued Cheyenne. 'I sure owe that galoot a heap of thanks,' thought the agent as he stumbled along towards the livery stable.

He rode out of town carrying saddle and bridle on his arm, guiding his mount by the pressure of his knees only. He wasn't wasting precious seconds in harnessing his horse when any moment those killers might catch up with him.

As he galloped past the hide merchant's office, he looked in at the open door. Sitting there in the yellow lamplight back of the table was Captain Galbray. He was writing.

The way he looked no one would have thought that he was planning the death of Joe Shay.

Cheyenne Joe didn't, anyway, riding past for Galbray looked his usual unemotional self, scratching away with the old-fashioned quill pen that was all a writer could get so far west along the frontier.

He bedded down in a hollow by the Smoky for the last few hours of night, but was mounted and away with early dawn. He found the place where the commanding officer had withdrawn his troops – it was a big ranch-house near to town and his men were bivouaced among the trees all around it.

Cheyenne rode through the lines of tents. They were being hastily struck, and there was every sign of a move imminent. Shirt-sleeved men were loading the quarter-master's wagons, the field guns were being wheeled on their limbers into a position on the roadside, while the cavalry units were already bringing their horses in from night pastures.

Cheyenne hastened his mount. He wanted to speak with the commanding officer before he grew too busy to see him. He found the major still at breakfast, and was allowed in immediately to speak with him.

He was an old man, so far as infantry officers went. A man nearer fifty than forty, heavy-built, shrewd-looking, with a face that looked not unkind.

The major looked up at him as he entered. There was some correspondence by the side of his plate. He said, 'Good-morning, Shay.'

Cheyenne returned the greeting. He spoke bluntly, because time was short. 'Last night I went to Captain Galbray and asked for help because four men were followin' me through the town, tryin' to kill me.'

The major's eyebrows bushed together. 'Why were they trying to kill you?'

'I caught them torturin' an Injun a couple of weeks ago. They were in the party that massacred them Injuns up Sycamore Creek.'

'What did the captain do?'

Cheyenne looked suspiciously at the major when he spoke. There was something in the way he said it that was disturbing, almost as if there was irony in his voice.

'He pulled a gun on me an' tried to make me march out to where them blasted killers was waitin' for me.'

The major sat back in his chair, his eyes hard. 'That's a curious charge – and a serious one – to make against a United States officer, Shay. Are you sure you know what you're talking about?'

Cheyenne nodded. 'Reckon I do, major.' His eyes were hard, too. There was something in the major's manner that jarred – a hostility that was beginning to be apparent. Of course all these army officers always stood by each other and wouldn't listen to tales against their kind. What he was saying would antagonize the major, of course after all, he had no one to corroborate his word, or anything with which to substantiate his charges. But he had to make a formal protest, so that it went on record, then if anything happened to him of a suspicious nature, attention might be diverted to his charges against the captain.

He hadn't expected to be believed, but all the same he hadn't expected antagonism before the name of Galbray was even brought into incriminating light. And yet he was sure that right from his first words this major had been hostile towards him.

'Galbray,' said Cheyenne bluntly, arguing that he had nothing to lose by telling the truth, 'was in charge of an escort to an Indian commissioner bringin' a hundred thousand dollars for Cheyenne bounty. That bounty never reached the Cheyennes. I have no doubts myself that Captain Galbray and the Indian commissioner conspired to keep at least part of that money for themselves.'

The major's eyebrows seemed to jerk a little, then his hand reached out and he began to read from a letter. His voice was cold, yet there was a sarcastic note to it as he read:

' "I have reason to believe that Indian agent Joe Shay has been playing a double game with the Cheyenne Indians. I believe him to be a renegade, who led some breeds in an attack which resulted in the loss of a wagon containing a bounty of one hundred thousand dollars, destined to keep the peace with the Cheyenne Indians.

'I have witnesses whom I can bring forward to testify against this man, and in my own mind I have no doubt that after hearing them you will order Shay to be shot out of hand.

' "May I ask that if Shay appears anywhere within your command you have him arrested and returned to me here, in the town of Ephraim, for trial and justice according to his deserts." '

The major lifted his head as he laid down the letter. 'The signature is that of Captain Jules Galbray, of the 7th United States Cavalry,' he said grimly. 'Now what have

102

you got to say about that, Shay?'

'I think Galbray a very smart man.' Shay admitted.
'But he's a liar, too.'

He lifted his eyes. The major was coming heavily to his
feet. 'I have men stationed outside this door, Shay,' he told
him. 'They will take you under arrest back to Ephraim.'

'Back to Galbray?' It startled him, to think that he was
to be taken and placed in the power of a man who feared
him and would accordingly take any measures to quieten
him. He began to protest, but the major lifted his hand to
silence him.

He said, 'This is nothing to do with me, Shay. I have
been asked to return you to Ephraim. I'm going to do it.
While this campaign is on I have no time to attend to – er
– such minor affairs. I have every confidence in Captain
Galbray, in spite of your charges. I have known him for a
long time, and he has always been a perfectly honourable
man and a good officer.'

And then he added, 'I'm surprised at this, Shay. You
know, you have an astonishing reputation as a mediator
with warring Indians. You're respected and trusted.' He
gestured helplessly with his hands. 'And then – this
happens.' And his manner said, 'Why do men do these
things? Why do even the most honourable suddenly turn
completely against character and perform the most
wretched of crimes?'

Cheyenne listened, heard the regret in the kindly
major's voice, and knew that his story wasn't believed.
Tradition was too strong with the major – Captain
Galbray was a brother officer, and as such was above
suspicion in the older man's mind.

A horse strayed across in front of the window, restless
at the unusualness of freedom while yet saddled.

Cheyenne's eyes followed it, and yet saw nothing. He
heard the major call, 'Sergeant!' And then three blue-
uniformed men came quickly into the room. One was an
untidy old sergeant, the other two troopers.

Cheyenne didn't look at them. He was thinking how

like his own horse that was, straying under the window. But he'd left his horse securely hitched to the rail round the front of the ranch-house.

The major said, briskly, suddenly very military. 'Sergeant, place this man under close arrest and send him under heavy escort back to Ephraim, to be put in charge of Captain Galbray.'

The sergeant saluted. He shouted an order. There was no need to shout in a room as small as that, but it is a way of sergeants, especially in the presence of a superior officer.

The two troopers immediately jumped, one to each side of the former Indian agent. Yet still Cheyenne didn't look at them because of the astonishing realization that that was his horse, straying right below the open window.

Only dimly, then did he hear a new voice.

'Sir!'

The major looked at the speaker in surprise. 'Well, Trooper?'

'I wish to be excused from acting as escort to Joe Shay.'

The words were like a bombshell in that room. The major's mouth dropped open in astonishment. Joe Shay wheeled – and saw Trooper Cole Newark. The sergeant took a deep breath and began, 'The hell, an' he volunteered—'

The young trooper faced his superior officer with astonishing composure. 'I was escort under Captain Galbray when Commissioner Pengelly went through this way with the Cheyenne bounty of a hundred thousand dollars.'

'What's that got to do with this matter, trooper?' barked the major. He was incensed. He had never heard of such talk before from a trooper on duty.

'Only that I think that if anyone investigated into the disappearance of that bounty at the scene of the supposed Indian attack—' Cheyenne suddenly cottoned on. The trooper wasn't looking at him, but all the same he was talking to him, telling him what to do – urging a plan of action on to him. He wasn't looking at Cheyenne, but for that matter he wasn't looking at the major.

He was looking straight out at that straying horse just outside the open window.

Cheyenne suddenly got it – a lot, anyway. That shot from the window – those rifle shots at the swinging lamps to that saloon. It must have been this gallant young trooper, trying to help him – he must have been following him around, on hand when he was required. Cheyenne suddenly blessed his chance meeting with the lad.

And now the boy must have unhitched his horse and brought it to a place convenient for flight – now he was telling him to get out through that window and make his escape from the military.

But how? With three other armed men in the room.

Cole Newark, still very calmly, had continued talking, had completed his sentence and was saying even more.

'—they might find something suspicious about that ambush. I reckon it's the queerest bit of Injun warfare I've ever heard tell of. Only one person seems to have seen Injuns – Captain Galbray.'

The major stopped him. 'Enough of that, trooper.' His face was grim, yet he was well-intentioned. 'If I let you go on I can see that I shall have to place you under arrest, too.'

Trooper Newark said, with composure. 'I am making no charges against Captain Galbray, sir.' Cheyenne thought, 'No, this kid's no fool.'

'But I'm saying that if Joe Shay is taken into Ephraim he will never come out of the place alive. There are desperate men in that town who want to close his mouth.'

Cheyenne felt a boot touch his left foot. It just touched, that was all, yet to Cheyenne it came clearly through as an urge for him get moving – pronto!

He took a chance and jumped for the window. Surprised, he heard Newark shout, 'Come back, you fool! Don't try to run away!' And Newark was clawing at his back as he went out through the window.

Then he realized what the boy's game was. While the boy was riding his back, no one could open fire on him. And also it cleared the boy of a charge of being complicit in his escape – it was good acting and must have looked like a genuine attempt to prevent him from escaping.

Admiration rose within him for the bold young trooper, even at that hazardous moment. He was certainly prepared to take risks when he considered that injustice was being done. He only hoped that the boy wouldn't suffer for trying to help him.

Cheyenne lent colour to the performance with a vicious snarl and an abrupt hand-off that flattened the boy's face. He knew the kid wouldn't mind. That freed him and he was out of the window and into the saddle in no time.

They started firing at him within seconds of his horse beginning to gallop, but all had been carrying sidearms only, and revolver bullets don't carry far. He got hit with a spent bullet that caught him in the middle of the back; it knocked some wind out of him, but didn't penetrate his clothing, and that was as near as they got to killing him.

There were sentries with rifles down the lane, but Cheyenne put his horse to a fence and got away round a copse of blackthorn and scrub oaks. Once his horse was in its stride he had no fears of being caught by any military pursuit. Soldiers had heavier saddles and equipment and their horses were bigger and heavier than his own and built for stamina and not for speed.

He took to a winding hill trail, knowing that a long ascent more than anything would blow the cavalry mounts with their greater burdens, and after the first five minutes he never saw a pursuer.

Accordingly, he took his time when he came out on a wooded brow, and let his horse walk. He sat alert, however, listening for any sound that would herald the arrival of the soldiers, but none came. He decided they must have followed a wrong track.

He sighed with relief at the thought. That was one thing, anyway. He was free, and that was better than being taken into Ephraim and put at the mercy of that sharp-faced army captain.

But his thoughts were far from happy as he sat under those trees, with the sunshine dappling his face and body as the slight breeze stirred the leaves and let the light fall on him.

He was an outlaw now. He couldn't go east because the United States army, in force now over hundreds of square miles of country, wanted him - and wanted him badly now. And westwards were the defeated Indians who would kill him because they hated him.

His position was not enviable, and he gave a lot of thought to his plans for the immediate future. What the boy trooper had hinted at wasn't something to be undertaken lightly. To go in and find that burnt-out wagon and look for clues as to what had really happened in that Indian 'attack' was a very dangerous undertaking. The boy said that the wagon had been burnt out at a place half a day's journey into Cheyenne territory. As the Indians were still roaming for miles east of Massacre, it meant that he would have to penetrate at least thirty miles into hostile territory.

Now as he sat his horse in the coolness under the trees, he tried to figure out his chances of survival if he undertook the expedition. They weren't good odds.

And then the steel came back into his grey eyes; the old determination wiped away the lines of indecision around his mouth. He urged his horse forward and turned its head - westwards.

He was prepared to take a chance on survival. The boy was right. If he could find evidence to prove that Galbray had faked an attack on that bounty wagon, then he might at least be able to return to his kind without the brand of outlaw attached to him.

So he set off towards Cheyenne territory, and at exactly that moment Commissioner Wade Pengelly, his head still sore from the fall the previous night, got the support of a mob of hard-eyed, vicious Kansas volunteers to follow him in an expedition into the territory.

And though the object of the expedition was declared to be the extermination of every Indian on the reservation, yet the route he chose for his ruffianly band was one which would bring him along the old trail now blocked by a burnt-out wagon.

CHAPTER EIGHT

THE ARROYO!

It took Cheyenne two days to cover those thirty miles, and he probably only succeeded in getting through because he took off his shirt and disguised himself as an Indian. At any rate, he tied his bandanna round his head, and from a distance, clad only in his buckskin trousers, he must have looked like a solitary Indian.

He saw several war-parties, and on at least one occasion was seen in return. He was riding along the face of a long, grassy ridge when he saw a dozen braves below him. They looked up at him, but made no attempt to ride after him. Probably they thought he was some wounded warrior returning to his village.

In fact, it proved unexpectedly easy to get through the old trail beyond the burnt-out town of Massacre. That was because any Indians in this territory believed it to be free of white men and so never suspected his presence there.

He wondered, however, if it would be so easy going back. The pressing forces of the United States army would by now be concentrating the defeated Indians into this area, so that on his return he could expect to run into more numerous parties of retiring warriors. He dismissed the thought with a shrug. Tomorrow would have to look after itself. When he came on to the old trail into the territory he moved with the greatest circumspection, for now he was riding right into the heart of enemy country - into the land of his old friends, he thought, with slight bitterness.

It took him a long time to cover those last few miles, because he never moved from cover until he had examined all the ground up to the next cover and was sure it was free from lurking enemies.

But in the end he came out on a hill overlooking the trail and saw below him the burnt remains of the commissioner's covered wagon. He tied his horse within the shelter of some sour-smelling elder bushes and went cautiously down to the wreck on foot.

The horses were dead in their harness. They had suffered from the fire, but when Cheyenne examined them he saw that all had been shot through the head. That could mean anything, of course. They could have been shot in an attack by Indians. Only, it was unusual to find four horses so neatly dispatched in the same place.

Then he went rooting round in the debris, among the charred ends of wood and white ashes. He was looking for the metal guards that had been clamped around the corners of the chest which had contained the bounty. And he found them.

That was a grievous disappointment to the agent. Vaguely he hadn't expected to find evidence that the chest really had been burned, but it looked as though that was the case.

He sighed. If the chest and the bounty had gone up in smoke he couldn't see that there was ever the chance of proving a conspiracy to defraud the government by stealing the bounty. They must have grabbed as much as they could carry, and had been satisfied with that.

It was very disappointing, and he went, feeling dejected, back to where his horse was tied in among the elders. It was a stinking place to stay, because green elder is rank and unpleasant especially in a thick coppice such as this: but then for that reason it wasn't likely to be visited by other people.

He sat down behind a screen of new-green stems and looked down upon the burnt-out wagon. It didn't fit, somehow, that men of Pengelly's stamp should be satisfied with a handful of money and deliberately burn the greater part of the bounty in an effort to hide evidence of the crime they had committed.

And yet, even if it didn't fit, he couldn't see what he could do about it. There was no ray of light to shine through his mental darkness just then.

He stayed around that elder clump for the next two hours. Having come so far he felt that he couldn't leave the vicinity of the crime without making every possible effort to get evidence to incriminate the crooks, yet he just didn't know where to begin.

And then an Indian came riding down the valley, a solitary brave who looked to have been severely wounded in the fighting, for he could hardly keep his seat on his mount. Almost immediately afterwards Cheyenne thought he heard the sound of distant firing. A few minutes later he was certain.

North and east of his position, over the rolling, wooded hill-top, a battle sounded to be raging, and it was coming nearer.

Cheyenne's immediate thought was: 'The Volunteers!' He knew that the United States army weren't likely to come so deeply into the reservation, and he guessed that the unscrupulous Pengelly must have had his way and urged the Volunteers into this reckless enterprise.

After a time Cheyenne began to see signs of battle high up on the hillside before him. Indians were streaming in full flight through the trees, sometimes hiding up so as to catch their enemies unawares and make a fight of it, but mostly going west as fast as they could. It was all too apparent that the Cheyenne might have been completely broken. They had got nowhere against the better-armed white man.

Then Cheyenne began to see the victorious Volunteers as they came riding over the crest, guns blazing white smoke as they pressed hard after the Indians. All in a

111

moment it seemed that the hillside above was alive with them - and Cheyenne felt none the safer for that.

But they weren't coming down into the valley where the old trail was. The battle was streaming westwards, and going away rapidly, and it reminded Cheyenne of the hunt he had seen with dogs when he was a youth and living in settled Virginia.

He had a feeling that he should be going, in case some skirmishing party stumbled on his hide-out; and then he saw movement among the bushes a hundred yards north of the burnt-out wagon and close to some old oaks. After a time he realized that three braves were crawling cautiously through the cover, intent, apparently, on getting out on to the trail.

Then they stopped and disappeared from sight among the thick grasses that were turning yellow under the heat from the summer sun. Cheyenne watched, wondering what they were up to, and surprised that they should so suddenly go into cover. He wondered if perhaps he had been incautious, and they had seen him and suspected him to be an enemy.

And then he saw Commissioner Pengelly and two blue-uniformed soldiers riding down the trail.

He nearly gave himself away at that in excitement. Pengelly and two soldiers returning to the burnt-out wagon - slipping back after the fighting had driven the Indians out of the district - two soldiers; maybe the two who had been in the plot to rob the wagon, the no-goods that the boy trooper had spoken about.

Maybe the same men that had killed the old Kentuckian.

And all in one moment Cheyenne understood the whole situation.

Pengelly was on his way back to recover the loot. It hadn't been burnt, only the chest in which it had been contained.

They must have hidden the money away, all but for a comparative handful, fearful of the consequences if they

were seen carrying so much money after the disappearance of the bounty. They had intended to come back into
the territory when it was safe for them to do so - safe, that
is, from suspicious white men's eyes.

But almost at once the hiding-place had been overrun
by hostile Indians. That was something they had never
reckoned on; that when they wanted to return for their
loot, they would be unable to do so.

Cheyenne understood now why Pengelly had urged the
Volunteers to smash right through the territory. If the
white men simply stood outside the territory after driving
the red men back, he would hardly be able to enter and
look for his hidden loot - not for some time, anyway. So,
completely unscrupulous, unheeding of the consequences
to anyone else, he had encouraged the Volunteers to ride
into the territory and thus give him chance of slipping
away and regaining the loot.

He took off the safety catch of his Sharps and waited,
his body tensed as he watched the approach of the white
men. Then his eyes switched to where he had last seen the
red men, but again this time he couldn't spot them. For all
he knew, they might have slipped away at sight of their
mounted enemies.

Pengelly was looking round him all the time from his
saddle. He wasn't a nervous man, but it it was plain that
he didn't want to be seen in his next actions.

The three men didn't hesitate. They all rode near to the
wagon and then branched off north, heading directly
towards the last place where Cheyenne had seen the
three lurking braves.

They came under the first of the oaks and reined in.
They were looking upwards, into the thick-leaved tree –
and that look completed the story so far as Cheyenne was
concerned.

One of the soldiers stood on his saddle and cautiously
straightened himself. His hands were reaching upwards;
were fumbling among the branches. The other two were
keeping watch.

Cheyenne thought: 'If they get away with that bounty I'll never be able to pin a case against them fellars.' So he put the rifle to his shoulder, determined to stop them from getting away with their loot.

Deliberately he fired into the branches above the soldier's head. At which exact moment three braves leapt from cover and raced towards the mounted men.

The loud report from the Sharps startled everyone, including the Indians. Cheyenne saw them hesitate for a fraction of a second; then they must have realized that the bullet was not intended for themselves, and that gave them greater courage.

Cheyenne rammed another round into the breech just as the startled soldier fell off his saddle. His horse had reared at the sound and thrown him, and now riderless, it came galloping furiously across the trail towards the green elders.

Pengelly bellowed something. Cheyenne didn't hear the words plainly enough to distinguish them, but he guessed what the commissioner was shouting: 'It's a trap! Get out of here!'

He went racing off eastwards, followed by one of the soldiers. The Indians, balked of the horses they had evidently designed to catch, fell on the second soldier and killed him.

Then they stood and looked across the valley towards the spot from which the shot had come, and Cheyenne could see them talking together, doubtful as to what they should do next.

The riderless horse had gone racing round the sprawling clump of elders, so that it was out of sight of the Indians below; but in circling it had got wind of Cheyenne's horse, even above the rank unpleasant smell of the elders, and after a time, trembling violently, it circled and started to come back towards the bushes.

The Indians couldn't make it out. Someone not hostile to them had fired from cover up on that opposite hillside, but with the departure of the two white men the rifleman had not emerged, as they had expected him to do.

After a hurried debate, the three started to run west-wards up the trail. They had probably reasoned that the rifleman must have gone away, perhaps in pursuit of the white men, for why otherwise didn't he show himself?

Cheyenne rose quickly and took a lot of risks as soon as the Indians were out of sight. If he wasn't a Dutchman he was pretty certain that Pengelly and his companion wouldn't be long in making another attempt to recover the loot, so he had to work fast.

That second horse, belonging to the dead soldier, was just what he needed; for he guessed that the major part of the loot would still be here, and it would probably weigh several hundred pounds. Payment to Indians was always made in small denominational bills, and tens of thousands of them were quite heavy.

But it proved exasperating, trying to catch that nervous beast, and it took Cheyenne a precious ten minutes before at last he seized the rein and secured the beast. Then he rode down with it to the old oak across the trail.

That was where he had to take many risks, for he was exposed all the time, just as Pengelly and his party had been exposed. But he was careless of safety at the moment. The prize was within his grasp - the evidence that would clear his name and at the same time incriminate the real miscreants.

Securely tied to the branches he saw half a dozen stout waterproof canvas bags. By the look of it, Pengelly had worked out everything right to the last detail.

Cheyenne whipped out his keen-edged Bowie - that knife that had caused him so much suffering - and hacked through the ropes. The bags were heavy, and it was precarious work, pulling them off the branches and drop-ping them to the ground without coming tumbling down himself. But in time it was done. In time the whole loot was distributed between his horse and the dead soldier's, with most of it going on the latter, of course.

He was sweating furiously with his exertions under that hot sun, and his heart was pounding furiously in expectation of discovery at any moment.

And yet he got away. He led the horses up behind the elders again and took to the wild country south of the trail. And less than an hour after he had gone Pengelly and his companion made a cautious return - and found the loot gone.

Pengelly lost his smoothness, lost all his charm and easy smiles, and raved like a maniac. For months he had worked to ingratiate himself with the Indian Office back in Washington; for months he had planned to turn his promotion to Indian commissioner into terms of hard cash. And his plan had worked perfectly, right until the unexpected Indian uprising - and now he had lost all that he had so cunningly schemed to get.

The soldier took the blow more phlegmatically, even though he was now a deserter from the army and appeared unlikely to get anything for all the grave steps he had taken. He hunted around for a sign, and at last showed tracks to Pengelly that led across the valley.

'Two hosses,' the trooper said. He looked at the deep imprints. 'Reckon the fellars went off pretty heavily laden!'

Pengelly looked up the hillside after the tracks. 'Then I reckon we can soon catch up with 'em.' He looked at the sun. 'They can't be more'n an hour ahead of us, an' I reckon to be up with 'em long before dark!'

But they weren't. They were up against a man skilled in Indian ways, and when they came to the first stream they lost his trail completely.

Yet they knew one thing. The men (as they thought) they were after weren't Indians but whites, because the general direction of that first trail was eastwards, out of the reservation.

Cheyenne never stopped travelling all that night. Now that he had the evidence against Pengelly and the captain of the escort, he couldn't rest until it was safely in the

116

hands of the major down near Ephraim. That would clear him of the charges against him, at the same time pinning the lie to Galbray.

By noon the following day, both horses were in a bad way, because he had come by the most direct route across the hills, and it was rough going and made especially tiring because of the darkness. Shortly after noon he ran into a company of infantry. He made no attempt to avoid them, and when he came up with them the lieutenant in charge recognized him.

At once he shouted an order, and immediately several men jumped forward and caught hold of the horses. The lieutenant, eyes narrowed against the sun, rapped: 'You're Joe Shay, aren't you? Yeah? Well, consider yourself under arrest.'

Cheyenne said drily that he didn't mind being under arrest. 'It suits me, lootenant. All I want is to get to your commanding officer as quickly as possible.'

That made the lieutenant suspicious, and he started to ask questions. Cheyenne didn't answer them. He didn't want to reveal that he had the better part of a hundred thousand dollars on his two horses, because soldiers were generally rough characters and it would have been a sore temptation to many of them.

A sergeant and two men were detailed to go with him back to the major's headquarters. These had been moved to a position south of Massacre by now, so that meant they had so many less miles to travel than Cheyenne had reckoned on. He was glad of it, for himself as well as his horses.

He felt safer too, travelling with an escort, because there were a lot of marauding bands roaming the countryside in search of loot – stragglers from the Hundred Day Volunteers, mainly – and two laden horses might have caused interest among them.

Two hours later they saw a tented camp down an arroyo and knew they had reached their destination. The sergeant in charge wanted to be officious and have him ceremoniously handed over to the guard commander, but Cheyenne got brusque, told him not to be a fool, and demanded to see the major without loss of time. In the end he got his way, as he so often did.

The major was in his tent, receiving reports and dispatching troops appropriately to those areas still infested with Indians. He was impatient at the interruption until he saw Cheyenne Joe between the escort, and then a smile of grim satisfaction came to his face.

'So they caught up with you,' he said pleasantly.

Cheyenne shook his head.

'No, sir. I was on my way to you when I ran into a lieutenant with infantry. I allowed myself to be arrested. I could have avoided your men if I had wanted.'

The major looked at the sergeant and lifted his eyebrows. The sergeant nodded. 'That's true, sir. His hosses were tired, but I don't reckon we could have caught up with him if he had wanted to avoid us.'

That brought a frown to the major's face. This wasn't consistent with his theory that Cheyenne was a renegade and an outlaw and as such would try to avoid the military. So he asked: 'What brings you here, Shay?'

'The better part of a hundred thousand dollars. I've got 'em in them packs on my two hosses.'

'You mean you've recovered the bounty money?'

'Most of it, I guess. I found it up a tree where it had been hidden.'

'Hidden?' said the major softly. 'By whom? You, Shay?'

'If I'd hidden it up a tree I wouldn't go an' get it an' bring it back to you,' Cheyenne retorted. 'Nope. I think you should ask Captain Galbray about this, an' Commissioner Pengelly, if you c'n find him.'

He remembered something.

'If you look at that lead horse of mine out there you'll find the army brand on it. The trooper who rode it last won't need it any more - he's dead. Two of your troopers deserted in the last day, I reckon. They were the two who went with Pengelly an' Galbray when the other escort

118

were sent back to look for Injuns.'

'You mean, those two troopers along with the commissioner and Captain Galbray alone know the truth of the attack on the wagon?'

'Just that. Wal, you'll find one of them troopers lyin dead within a hundred yards of the burnt-out wagon. It don't prove nothin', but you ask yourself why a trooper should desert in the face of the enemy - which carries the penalty of death - in order to trek back to a burnt-out wagon.'

'Yes,' said the major thoughtfully. 'It does kinda incriminate his companions at the time of the supposed attack.'

Cheyenne heard that word 'supposed' and knew that his story was believed. His heart jumped with delight, then he began to look ahead to think of the next move he had planned to make. He had to free himself from the stigma of being a hunted outlaw first, and then—

Bluntly he demanded: 'What does this make me, major? Am I still a wanted man or am I free?'

'You're not free, not yet, Shay.' Cheyenne's heart sank. 'I feel your story has something to support it, but until I can confirm your various statements - such as that one of my deserters is in fact dead alongside that burnt-out wagon - you will have to remain under arrest.'

Cheyenne was bitterly disappointed and his face showed it. He sank down, uninvited, on to an ammunition box and spoke straight out to the major.

'I don't want to be under arrest. I want to be free to undertake a mission into Cheyenne territory, with the idea of putting an end to this war, major.'

There was no mistaking the sincerity in the former Indian agent's voice as he made his appeal.

'I hate war, major, passionately. I've seen too much of it, and I've never seen it do anyone any good. But things are happenin' just now that are worse than war. When I was inside Cheyenne territory, lookin' for this bounty, I saw a sight that sickened me.'

The major asked: 'What was it, Shay?' His eyes never left the strong, brown face before him. He seemed to be fascinated by the manner of the man who was speaking to him.

'I saw an array of white, men - Kansas Volunteers, I reckon - shootin' their way into Cheyenne territory. They'd been inflamed into doin' this by bad talk from Pengelly. I heard it, back in Ephraim one night. He wanted to get 'em into Cheyenne territory so that it would be safe for him to collect the bounty money he'd hidden. So he began to get 'em worked up with talks of wipin' out all Injuns on the reservation.'

'Did he?' The major sat back, his face hard and angry. 'I gave orders that the border line of the Cheyenne territory should not be crossed.' He looked quickly at Cheyenne. 'I'm a soldier, Shay, but I don't like unnecessary bloodshed, either. I figgered if the Indians went back to their villages we could sit an' talk about responsibility and punishment afterwards. Killing women and children never did solve anything.'

Cheyenne said: 'I'm glad to hear it.' And his heart warmed towards the older man. He said: 'Wal, Major, the Volunteers ignored your order, an' now they're right in the heart of Cheyenne territory. How're you goin' to stop 'em before they get to the villages an' do as they threaten?'

The major sat in silence, his eyes downcast and brooding. After a long silence he looked again at Cheyenne Joe and his eyes were without hope.

'I don't see what I can do,' he said slowly. 'I can send messengers with orders for them to come out of the territory—'

'But you know they won't take any notice of messengers.'

'Yes, I'm afraid so.'

So Cheyenne Joe told of the plan that had been developing in his mind on his way in to see the major.

'I'll need my freedom for it,' he said bluntly. 'I want to

go to meet the Cheyenne chiefs an' talk 'em into a cease fire.'

'Aren't you taking a risk?'

Cheyenne didn't answer that question. Even the major didn't realize what a risk he took in showing himself to his former friends. But Cheyenne was prepared to take any risk, so long as it stopped this awful slaughter that was threatened.

'I want to take an offer to the Injuns, major - an offer from you.'

'And that is?'

'If the Injuns will allow your men safe conduct into the territory, you will put them between the Injuns an' the Volunteers an' drive 'em out of the territory. I want your word that you'll do that, an' havin' done it that you an' your men will retire to the border line while peace terms are formally discussed.'

The major was rising to his feet while Cheyenne was speaking. There was excitement in his face, and it was flushed now and his eyes were bright. 'Shay, if you could do this—'

Cheyenne Joe rose to face him.

'I'll do my best, major. I'll do anythin' in order to stop this bloodshed.' He paused, then said: 'Do I get my freedom, sir?'

The major hesitated, looking intently at him. Then he said: 'I'll take a risk, too, Shay. You may be spinning me a yarn just to escape again from me. If events prove that to be so, then I suppose I'll be drummed out of the service. But I want this war to end as humanely as possible, so I am prepared to take a risk, too.'

He held out his hand. 'Go, Shay. Good luck - and don't let me down.'

Cheyenne said: 'After that I can't let you down, major. Now, I want a fast horse, as mine is in need of rest. An' I want you to move your men right up to the Allardyce Springs on the borders of Cheyenne territory. If I'm successful, you'll be sent for.'

121

Half an hour later he rode out from that arroyo, heading west towards the fighting - and the Indian maiden named Blue Flower.

CHAPTER NINE

THE ROPE!

He rode hard, because he knew there was little time if he were to achieve his objective. He must arrange for a truce so that the military could move into the territory and protect the Indians from their blood-lusting enemies.

It was a curious role for the army, but he had confidence in that kindly old major and he felt sure he would keep his word and prevent the Cheyennes from being annihilated.

Cheyenne didn't feel bitterness or hatred against the Volunteers, either - only abhorrence for what they contemplated doing. He knew the type of men they were, for all his life he had lived with them.

They had been brought up to live defensively, like wild animals, ever ready to hurt when they were hurt, to kill if their lives were threatened. An eye for an eye, and a tooth for a tooth - that was the code of too many on the frontier at that time.

But men like Cheyenne Joe Shay - and now, it seemed, that grey-haired major - were no longer content to live in such a primitive state. Such men urged settlement by words and not by blows, and all over the west their influence was beginning to be felt.

Joe Shay had once been one of the most influential peace makers, but he knew now that he had lost his old influence with the tribes. Now, if they were to listen to him, he would have to start again to win their confidence, and he wasn't so sure that his enemies in their ranks would let him speak out.

He rode on and ignored these thoughts of the appalling danger into which he was thrusting himself. He was prepared to risk his life in an effort to save the lives of the defenceless and bring order to the territory again.

That night he slept because clouds obscured the moon and he could not see to ride in safety. It fretted his spirit, but all the same the rest was needed and it did him good. He was away with dawn, following in the tracks of the victorious Volunteers.

It was apparent, though, that the men from Kansas hadn't found everything to suit them. Cheyenne saw signs where dead had been buried, and evidence of vicious fighting in the wooded hill country that was so suitable for Indian warfare. The Indians plainly were putting up the maximum resistance in an effort to save their people.

It gave Cheyenne a chance with his plan, but he knew that it would rouse the frustrated Volunteers to further heights of vindictiveness, and he kept going at his best pace all that day.

On several occasions he came across wounded, either heading back for the settlements or lying up in pain, attending to each other's injuries. From these he began to get an idea of the way the fighting was going.

The Indians had been routed out on the plains, and though they were still in overwhelming numbers they had split up into bands that harried the better-armed Volunteers but were unable to threaten them seriously. The best they could do with their attacks was to slow down the advance of the Kansas men, and give their people a chance to escape from the awful fate threatening them.

Cheyenne also learned that the Indians had been headed off from retreat into the wild Sawash Mountains, and were being driven towards the Republican River, south of the territory. That put them no more than a day's riding from Allardyce Springs, Cheyenne calculated, and meant that if the Indians would agree to his proposal, the military would not be long in riding in to stop the slaughter.

When he received this information he struck south immediately, hoping to join up with the Indians. Instead, he ran into a strong body of Kansas men, preparing for a last foray before dark.

Nobody took any notice of Cheyenne when he suddenly rode down on them. There were lots of stragglers seeking to join up with the stronger forces. So, when he saw them preparing to mount and ride again, he pulled discreetly off the trial and struck off westwards so as to have the advantage of cover.

About a quarter of an hour after that he came across a band of Indians.

He was in the shelter of a small grove of trees, looking out for cover on a line south of him, when the first of a weary band of fugitives came plodding over a rise. There were about a couple of dozen people in all, mostly women and children, but with a few old men and some wounded braves among them.

They were without horses, and the women were dragging the wounded on litters. They seemed to be without burdens of any kind, probably having thrown everything aside when the mad pursuit started.

He stayed where he was until the terrified band came level with his hiding-place. The way they were going they would walk right into the posse of Volunteers, a mile or two east along the valley, and he wanted to warn them and turn them aside into safety.

So when they were within twenty yards of his hiding-place, he touched his horse's sides and rode out into their midst.

The children screamed in terror at seeing a hated white man, and clung to their mothers, while the women-folk broke into a terrified clamour and started to run away. Cheyenne shouted desperately:

'Don't run away! I won't harm you! Don't you remember me - Jo-shay, your friend?'

One of the wounded crawled painfully from his litter, knife in hand, and prepared to defend his people with his life. It was a gallant gesture.

Cheyenne dismounted, leaving his Sharps in the boot of his saddle, and strode across to the swaying, pain-racked brave. He came with his arms outstretched, showing that his hands were empty of weapons, and he walked deliberately until he was within a pace of the brave, so that if the man had wanted he could have stabbed the knife into him.

But Cheyenne was speaking as he walked, talking urgently. 'I am your friend. I come to warn you that you are walking into death. Ahead of you is a strong band of white men who will kill you if you continue down the valley.'

Then he was right up to the brave. And the brave didn't kill him.

Cheyenne knew the man. He wasn't a Strong Heart, and he didn't know his opinions on peace and war. But he said gently: 'It is an evil thing, this war, and I am riding to your chiefs to try to stop it.'

The brave still crouched before him, that lean brown hand gripping the short, straight dagger. His face was full of suspicion as he said: 'Jo-shay is no longer the friend of the Cheyenne. Jo-shay turned on the red man just as all other white men do.'

'We'll argue that later,' Joe Shay said tiredly. 'All you need to believe just now is that you're walkin' into a trap, an' I came out to warn you against it.'

At that moment weakness overcame the wounded man, and his legs collapsed beneath him. The women, standing in a frightened group, thirty or forty yards away, saw the white man bend over the brave and try to make him more comfortable in his pain. There was a gentleness about the action that spoke more than words to the suspicious little audience, and immediately all fear of the white man fled. They came crowding back around the former Indian agent.

He heard them talking quickly, excitedly, so many at once that when he wanted to speak his voice remained

126

unheard. He rose, accordingly, and held up his hands for quiet. Once again he was confident in the power of his appeal to these people.

When they were quiet he spoke tersely. 'Get off the trail. Take to the woods, or else you'll be discovered by a band of white men comin' up the valley, an' you won't live to see tomorrow. Hurry!'

He helped to put the wounded brave back on his litter and drag him up the hillside into the shelter of a belt of timber. The brave kept his head turned all the time to watch him, his dark face still filled with suspicion, his hand never relaxing its grip on that dagger.

But the women didn't seem to have any doubts about him. All in one second they had accepted him again, just as they had accepted him as a friend when he had been with the tribe. And the children whom he had known came and chattered excitedly to their old friend, Jo-shay.

When they were up the hillside some distance they came out into a clearing and were able to look down over the trees on to the valley trail they had just left.

Cheyenne Joe heard a shrill cry from one of the women. She was pointing down the hillside. He turned. Below them rode the Volunteers.

When he saw that Cheyenne Joe had spoken truly and had saved their lives, the wounded brave grunted and sank back in greater comfort on his litter. Cheyenne Joe was accepted by the warrior now, just as the squaws and the children had accepted him before. It made his heart lighter that he should have been able to make friends again with these Indians.

He wanted to leave them, having led them to safety for the moment, anyway. But they were afraid when he mentioned it and clamoured for him to stay with them and guard them with his rifle.

'I want to meet up with your chiefs as soon as I can,' he told them, but in the end he decided to keep with them until darkness, and then to travel on during the night to find the main body of Cheyennes. An old man said he thought he knew where the chiefs would be, and he would guide him there.

But a few minutes before darkness a war party of braves, led by Strong Hearts, came riding down and joined them.

The moment he saw those plumed headdresses bobbing through the undergrowth towards them, Cheyenne's heart seemed to stop beating. Now was the testing time. In a moment he would know if his gamble were to come off - or if he was going to die.

He brought the Sharps quickly out of the saddle holster. His intentions were good, so far as the Indians were concerned, but he was human enough to be ready to fight against them if they threatened his life.

They came bursting out of the bushes - saw him and stopped dead in their tracks. Cheyenne looked at the war bonnets, at the painted faces, hideous and brutalized by their recent experiences. And he saw little mercy in those eyes.

His rifle came up. That halted the warriors.

Then one of them spoke harshly, and for once Cheyenne didn't understand what he was saying. Immediately, though, a clamour arose from the little band that he had saved, and he heard voice after voice shout a protest against whatever had been said. They were indignant, these people, anxious to protect him because he had protected them.

And then the wounded brave behaved gallantly yet again. He rose from his litter and came and stood against Cheyenne, and again he was holding his knife, but this time the blade was not turned against the white man.

He raised his voice, though it was weak from pain, and he told those threatening braves: 'Jo-shay came and saved me and my squaw and my papooses. For that my life is his. Let no man raise a hand against him, for I must die rather than see him hurt.'

Cheyenne Joe put his arm round the brave to support him, but he spoke to the war-painted braves on their wild, foam-flecked little ponies. 'I am Jo-shay, your friend, and I come as always in peace. I come from the leader of the soldiers out on the plain, with a message for your chiefs. That message can bring peace to your tribe, and save your women and children - and yourselves - from terrible slaughter.'

But a brave rode forward and spoke harshly. He was a man who walked with a dragging foot, but rode superbly and was a warrior among warriors. But always he was bitter, perhaps because his lameness made him different from other men.

Now he shouted: 'You are a white man! Nothing good can come from listening to you. Yet again you are come among us to trick us. You, because your tongue speaks friendliness, are lower than those white men who scalp before our injured warriors are dead.'

And the thought of it seemed to fill him with fury and he came riding in at Cheyenne, his lance raised for the death thrust.

Chevenne's rifle lifted immediately to his shoulder as he prepared to defend himself. Yet even as he did so he was saying to himself, 'It didn't come off. This is the end!'

For if he tried to defend himself he was certain to be killed eventually - they were too many for him. And the other alternative - not even to try to save his life – wouldn't help the Indians.

But the wounded brave shouted something, and at once a woman ran across, holding her papoose before her, and stood in front of the white man. That stopped the lance thrust, for if the crippled warrior had tried to stab at Cheyenne he would only have hurt the woman or her child. The warrior with the dragging foot shouted angrily and pulled his horse's head around so as not to trample on the people clustering around the paleface.

He was furious at the opposition and railed at them from his horse, but the wounded brave gave back the same answer: 'My life is his, and my family's, too. We cannot in honour do anything but give our lives to save him.'

Other women and some of the old men now came up and stood protectively around Joe Shay. They were certainly showing their appreciation to the man who had saved their lives. The baffled cripple rode back to his friends and harangued them and tried to get them to help him remove the people so that they could get at the white man, but they seemed less vicious than he and made no move.

Cheyenne realized that they were tired and depressed with defeat, and no longer did it seem important to go on killing enemies - only to the warrior, whose twisted leg had twisted his brain, too, and made him morose and savage. Now those braves were concerned with saving their own lives and those of their loved ones; now they were seeing the folly of war.

So one spoke up. ' If Jo-shay is come in peace, then he should have chance to speak with our chiefs. Our enemies are close upon us, and we are powerless to stop them with our own puny weapons.'

'There speaks a woman,' shouted the lame warrior savagely. 'The white man is our hated enemy. Let us die rather than submit to him. There is no honour in living alongside a white man, but there is glory in death against the treacherous paleface.'

Not long ago those stirring sentences would have evoked a cheer from the braves, but not now. The evil of war had been brought home to them. The Indians had started this trouble, and now they only wished they could put an end to it.

So that other warrior said: 'There speaks a fool. Let him die if he wants to. We want to live so that we can look after our wives and children. If Jo-shay says he has a plan of peace, we will hear it.'

At that Cheyenne walked forward, leading his horse.

'I have a plan. If there is goodwill between us, we can stop this war within the next day and a half. Take me to your chiefs immediately, that I may be heard.'

The braves conferred together. Some clearly were suspicious of the white man's intentions, but a majority were in favour of leading him to their chiefs. A tall young brave announced the decision. 'We will take you, but you must give up yours arms to us. If this is a trap, you will die quickly.'

Cheyenne hesitated. To surrender his arms put him completely at the mercy of these savage-looking red men. He studied that painted face before him. The paint was to frighten enemies, but when Cheyenne looked through it he saw the lines of suffering, of weariness and disillusion. And the eyes were dull and without hope, but they looked straight and seemed the eyes of an honourable man.

He said, 'All right, my red brother, my head is in your hands. I will trust you.' For his experience with the Cheyennes had taught him that they were as honourable with their word as most white men - perhaps more so.

Slowly he unbuckled his belt and held it out along with the Sharps. The tall young brave took them, then stepped back. Cheyenne felt naked without his guns, and he was afraid, too, but he tried not to show it.

And then the war-painted braves seemed to lose interest in him, as if the gesture he had made in surrendering his guns had carried conviction with them. Cheyenne sighed with relief.

He had made friends with the women and children, then with a wounded brave. Now he seemed to have secured some of the old trust he had enjoyed from this party of warriors. His pulse beat faster at the thought that he was succeeding, that now he could approach the chiefs and the rest of the tribe with a feeling that he had some support behind him.

A few minutes later he thought to look for the lame warrior, but he was not to be seen. As they rode, though, he looked down on new-made tracks of a horse that had gone ahead of them. It was a horse galloping at speed. Cheyenne wondered if it was the lame warrior, and if so where he was going and what he was doing.

'Perhaps,' he thought, 'he's goin' to warn someone.' And immediately his thoughts jumped to White Fox and his supporters in the Strong Heart band. If that were true, then he could be sure of a troublesome time before him.

Cheyenne went ahead with a dozen braves, leaving the rest of the warriors to act as escort to the little band that Cheyenne had saved. Again the night was cloudy, after less than one hour of moon, and not even those sharp-eyed Indians could find their way over that rough country in the gloom of night.

They halted, for which their horses, anyway, were grateful, and rested until dawn, when they resumed their way. Shortly after daylight they began to see other groups of Indians, all heading in the same direction as themselves. Cheyenne realized that now he was in the heart of Indian territory, one white man in the midst of hundreds of enemies. And he was without arms.

The braves in those other parties were curious when they saw Jo-shay riding with their brethren, and came spurring across to know the reason why. Cheyenne could hear the harsh, grunting conversation in his rear, but he pretended indifference and never turned to see who was speaking.

There was a lot of argument, as some more vindictive than the rest counselled harsh measures against the man they had once trusted above all other men, yet who had appeared to betray them when they most needed him. Then it was that the tall young warrior and his companions proved themselves men of their word.

'We promised safety to the white man if he gave up his guns to us,' he heard them say. 'That is our word and we will keep it.'

Cheyenne was satisfied and ceased to worry now. He knew the Cheyennes and knew them to be an honourable people.

So it was that as they neared the camp of the Cheyenne tribe, their strength was swollen by newcomers until it seemed that Joe Shay was heading a procession. He didn't mind this. On the contrary it seemed an advantage to him, for it would seem at first sight as though he came to the chiefs with strong support among the warriors. Little things like that might be turned to good advantage.

Once he asked a question of the tall young warrior. 'My

good friend, Black Bear,' he said. 'How has he fared in this fighting?'

The warrior told him that his old friend was dead. 'He died when our braves came riding back to say that Joe Shay had led them into ambush, that the bounty wagon was not where you said it to be. Little Fox and his friends set on to him and killed him, remembering that it was Black Bear who had given you the hand of friendship and said his life was surety for what he was doing.'

'Dead,' whispered Cheyenne, and his heart smote him, for he felt that he was the cause of his good friend's death. 'He died for me, O Warrior. Black Bear was a man among men, and there will never be another like him.'

They rode in silence while Cheyenne nursed his grief, and then unexpectedly the warrior spoke - spoke without looking at him, as if perhaps ashamed of what he was saying.

'White Fox killed him not because of you, O Jo-shay, but because he saw in Black Bear a man who would always speak against war, and White Fox wanted scalps and would not rest content until he had his people riding the war trails again. That was why he killed him.'

Cheyenne said softly: 'O Warrior, I shall remember that in my grief you tried to console me.' But the warrior, bred to believe that softness was weakness, kept his eyes ahead and spoke no more.

In the early afternoon they found the main body of the tribe. They had taken refuge in a canyon which had only one entrance, and were preparing to fight to the death in it because they saw it was hopeless to attempt flight any more. Now they were weary, and they were burdened with many wounded, as well as their children and womenfolk.

There were few tepees on the grassy bottom of the valley, and the Cheyenne families were huddled forlornly in the shade from overhangs on the sheer cliff face. They took their misfortunes stoically, but it was plain that all saw only death in the end for them.

On the whole there was apathy as Cheyenne came

riding in, apathy because they had suffered so much in such a short time, and they seemed drained of emotion of any kind. But a few were there to stand up and call for death for this white man. Some were warriors, but a few were women who had lost their husbands in the fighting.

Cheyenne kept on without turning his head, though it hurt him to feel the concentration of hatred from those who shouted for his life. A group of chiefs came down from the foot of a red stone bluff to meet him as he rode up. Cheyenne looked among them and saw the white-painted face of White Fox, only White Fox was no longer a minor chieftain; now he was, by his plumes, a great chief and leader of men.

Then Cheyenne recognized that war bonnet and saw it was the one that Black Bear had worn until the peace treaty was made, and his temper rose within him. This man was not fit to wear the war bonnet of so great and noble a man as Black Bear!

The chiefs gave him greeting, and he raised his hand in return, and said 'How, my red brothers!'

The tall young warrior began to speak, but Cheyenne lifted his hand, and said: 'I can speak for myself.'

He dismounted and let his horse stray across to where Indian ponies were cropping the withering grass down in that hot valley. The chiefs stood in a group about a dozen yards from him, while all behind him the braves sat their horses to listen to what was being said.

Cheyenne came to the point. 'It was not the intention of the United States Army commander to pursue you into your territory. It was in his mind to push you back over the border and then to discuss peace terms with you.

'But there are men who have been inflamed against you.' Though the situation was perilous for him, yet even now he spoke his mind honestly and forthrightly. 'These men have seen their kind, even women and children, butchered by war-mad Indians, and they are in fierce anger against you and swear they will not rest until there is no Indian, of any age or sex, left upon the American continent.'

A savage growl arose at that statement. Cheyenne checked it quickly by lifting his hand. 'I am not here to discuss blame and to say what is to happen to the men responsible for this terrible, unnecessary war. I am here to try to save your lives, and I want you to listen to me.

'These men who have come on your heels into this reservation are even now following your trails and will surely catch up with you in a matter of hours. Against their rifles you cannot hope to last out for any great length of time, trapped here in this canyon.'

'Neither,' said a chieftain harshly, 'can we hope to escape by fleeing from them.'

'But there is one way of escape,' Cheyenne told them. 'The commander of the United States Army wishes for no more bloodshed, and if you will guarantee peace he will march with his men and drive back those Kansas Volunteers who come to kill you all. But there must be peace in your hearts - genuine peace. It is not sufficient to speak peace and then turn on the soldiers when they come to help you. If you promise peace now there must be an end to fighting until terms are discussed between you and the United States Army commander.'

He looked round, but those impassive faces gave no indication of the thoughts behind the war-paint. He felt that he was having an uphill struggle to convince these people that what he was saying was in their own interests.

He went on, trying to speak as if confident they would agree to his suggestion in the end.

'There are many bands of Indians still roaming between us and the place where the army now awaits your decision. If they see soldiers on Cheyenne territory they will fight bitterly against them, and will try to hold them back, just as others are trying to hold back the Volunteers.

'But that is not to your advantage. If the army is to get here in time to save your people, they must be given safe conduct through the territory.'

'What do you mean, safe conduct?' An old chieftain was

135

quick to seize upon his words.

'I mean,' said Cheyenne steadily, 'that a number of you chiefs must ride back with me so as to bring the army through without opposition from wandering bands of braves.'

White Fox bounded forward, his white-painted face hideous and savage. 'Do not listen to him!' he shouted. 'Do you not know by now of the duplicity of all white men and of Jo-Shay in particular? Do you not see that this is a cunning move to place our chiefs in the power of the white man's army? Let us kill this scheming dog!' he cried, and now his hand came up with a gleaming dagger and he made as if to stab at their old ally.

White Fox moved too quickly for others to intervene, and Joe had to grapple with him to save his own life. He caught hold of that slim, steel-strong wrist and held it away from him, while he glared into the distorted, painted face before him.

And suddenly Cheyenne Joe lost his temper with the cunning, scheming chieftain. Suddenly he felt so sick with everything that he didn't care what he said. All he knew was that this man was responsible for the deaths of hundreds of people - he had killed his old friend, Black Bear, and now sought to kill him, Joe Shay, too.

Fury gave him astonishing strength, as it often does. With a growl as savage as that of any Indian, he pulled hard on that wrist and at the same time jerked the Indian across his extended leg.

The knife fell out of White Fox's hand, while the chief crashed over on to his back.

He was up in an instant, however, jumping for the white man's throat. Cheyenne felt the fingers clawing at him, and then, for a few seconds, he went beserk. When he recovered it was to find himself standing over a bloody-faced, dazed White Fox, down in the dust at his feet.

He looked round. The chiefs and braves had watched the fight with interest, but had not attempted to interfere. As he sought to regain his breath and wiped the perspiration from his brow, he thought he understood.

These Indians had had enough of White Fox and his evil counsels. He had invited a thrashing, and he had got it.

Cheyenne said, 'Now will you discuss this while I rest? But whatever your answer is, let it come quickly, for there is little time if you are to be saved.'

He went across to where the shadows fell from the western wall of the canyon, and lay down, grateful to be out of the sun. He felt very weary, and he was sick from the exertions of the last few days. Perhaps, he thought, he had still not recovered his strength following the fever brought on by his wounded arm.

Idly he looked across to where White Fox lay in the dust. After a while the humbled chieftain got to his feet and walked slowly away down the valley. Even then there were men who followed him - perhaps too closely bound to his fortunes to want to desert him now. They passed out of sight.

Cheyenne thought, 'All the same, that fellar will do me no good if he gets the chance.'

Someone moved close to him. He looked up. Blue Flower was sitting a few yards away. His eyes dropped and he saw that the Indian girl had brought him food and water. He drank the water but left the food untouched. He had food in his saddle-bags, and these people must be short and he couldn't rob them of the little provisions they had.

He spoke to her. 'My heart is pleased at the sight of you, O Blue Flower. You bring me food and water, yet I thought you were my enemy, because you stood out and spoke against me.'

Abruptly she rose. 'All white men are my enemy,' she told him fiercely, and then suddenly she ran away.

Cheyenne watched her go, his eyes twinkling. 'All white men,' he thought, '- but not Joe Shay.' Because girls don't bring food and water to men they hate.

It seemed to bring strength into his veins, and he lost his feeling of weary hopelessness. Instead he rose and, impatient for action, strode across to the circle of chiefs and Strong Hearts who sat in counsel.

Some resented the interruption, but Cheyenne was past caring for niceties. 'You talk too much,' he told them bluntly. 'While you argue, your enemies come nearer and the fate of your women and children becomes more certain. Who are there among you who will risk their lives on my word, as I did on the word of a Cheyenne warrior?'

A Strong Heart growled, 'The last time men rode out with you, only two came back alive.'

'That was no fault of mine. It was the fault of White Fox and his followers who turned men's hearts against the red man wherever they were to be found. Your Strong Hearts were ambushed by white men who had just returned from Luther country and were in no mood to see red men so near to their settlements.'

An old, old chieftain, who had borne honour in his day but was long past fighting, now rose to his feet. He spoke impatiently. 'It is as Jo-shay says. There is no time for talk, but only for action. I am an old man, with little life left in me. If this is a trick of the white man's to get our scalps, they will not be pleased with my old thatch. I will put myself in Jo-shay's hands.' He looked at the white man. After a moment he said, 'I will trust him again. He was once our friend.'

Cheyenne Joe took his hand. It did him good to hear such words. Then other chiefs rose. Clearly none liked the mission, and most were suspicious of it. But they were brave men, prepared to risk their lives in an effort to save their families.

'We will go,' they said, and within minutes a body of six men rode out of the canyon - one white man, and five brave Indian chieftains.

Less than five minutes on their way, they came across a couple of wounded braves, riding together on one horse that was near to death itself. They told the party that the fierce Volunteers were less than five miles away, and massing their strength.

Even as the brave spoke, they began to hear distant

firing, echoing down among the hills. Now that the enemy was coming so close to their last retreat, bands of Indians would be fighting with the utmost savagery to hold back the white men as long as possible.

Cheyenne looked at the descending sun and thought, 'The Volunteers won't get to the canyon before dark.' That meant a night's peace, for it was unlikely that the men from Kansas would continue their attack during the hours of darkness.

He prayed for a moon, so that his party could continue all through the night, but his prayer was only partly answered. There was cloud to obscure the waning moon, so that often they had to feel their way forward in utter darkness for periods up to half an hour.

Fortunately they had made the long Allardyce Basin before nightfall, and they were able to continue, if haltingly, during the dark spells because they were able to follow the downward slope of the valley.

Dawn found them within eight miles of the Springs, and as the sun rose to help them they urged their horses into a mad pace in order to save precious minutes that might save precious lives.

They knew that, back in the hills behind them, the Kansas men would be pressing hard towards the canyon, perhaps by now might even be thronging the narrow mouth. The Indians would fight tenaciously, but in face of the superior weapons of the white man, they would be driven back. Then their last stand would break and the vengeful white men would pour in among them—

The Indian chieftain riding by his side looked grim and impassive, but Cheyenne knew that they were feeling just as desperate inside as he was. They loved their people just like any other men, and right now they would be praying to the Great Spirit to give them speed so that their families could be saved.

All at once the army camp came into view alongside the Springs. Men jumped to arms at sight of that careering bunch of Indians; then they saw Cheyenne and relaxed.

The major watched them come in and anticipated the message Cheyenne would give him. He turned and rapped out a series of orders. As Cheyenne and his party thundered up to the sentry posts, they heard a bugle sing out a call. They saw men racing to saddle their mounts; saw furious activity as two hundred troopers competed to be first to be ready. The major wasn't wasting time. He was a soldier who didn't like fighting, and was determined to stop this mad slaughter in the hills.

Cheyenne swung down from his saddle, exhausted. The Indians sat their mounts without attempting to alight, and their eyes were fierce and hard as they watched the closing ring of blue-uniformed enemies about them.

Then that gallant old major walked right in among them, bareheaded and unarmed. He carried a bowl of water and held it towards that old, old chieftian who had first placed his trust in Joe Shay. The old man took it with a dignified inclination of his head to express thanks; when he had drunk he passed it on to a companion.

The major said, 'You were successful, Shay?' Cheyenne Joe nodded. 'That was a good job well done,' said the major, and his grey eyes were alight with admiration, because he well knew what risks this man must have taken.

'The Volunteers have probably got the Cheyenne tribe trapped in a canyon now, sir,' he said, his chest heaving from the exertions of that long ride. 'There is no time to be lost if the Indians are to be saved.'

The major answered, 'When my men are ready, we will move out at once. I have two hundred cavalry - infantry would be too slow, so they are being kept here, at the Springs.'

Fresh horses were now brought up for Cheyenne and the chiefs. They were accepted with little grunts of approval. It was apparent that their suspicions were fast being removed by the courtesy of their treatment. Food was given them, and hurriedly consumed, and then a cavalry captain rode up, saluted, and announced that the men were ready to move out. Looking past him, Joe Shay

saw the grinning, cheerful face of Trooper Cole Newark.
He'd come out of things all right.

The major went across to his horse and mounted. He
gave a signal, and the bugler blew another ringing call,
and the cavalcade rode out from the Springs at a fast trot.
As they went, the infantry lined the way and gave them a
cheer to speed them on their way.

They rode steadily all that day. In all of them was that
feeling of impatience, of an illogical desire to kick heels
into their mounts and race their fastest to the aid of the
hard-pressed defenders. But all knew that if they pressed
their mounts too hard now they would founder on that
long, stony trail into the hills.

Late that afternoon found a long line of mounted
soldiers strung out on a winding path that climbed the
last of the hills before they reached the Cool Top Range
and the canyon. Long before they saw the rearing face of
those mighty bluffs on either side of the canyon, they
heard heavy rifle fire.

The major halted at the head of the pass. When
Cheyenne rode up he saw why. Close on a hundred
Indians, Shoshone as well as Cheyenne, were drawn up in
their path, ready to fly at the hated blue uniforms.
Cheyenne shouted, and immediately the chiefs came
racing out from behind him and ran their horses between
the two bodies of men.

The cavalry hastened their mounts, but the party was
vulnerable, strung out as they were, and if the Indians
had attacked they could have held the troopers for a
considerable time down that pass.

So it was with relief that they saw the chieftains ride
up to that strong force of Indians and begin to parley with
them. At least it gave them time to bring up their men
and group them at the head of the pass.

After a while one of the chiefs rode back and spoke to
Cheyenne. 'They will stand aside and let us go through.'
Cheyenne translated for the benefit of the major. The
major nodded and gave the order to march again.

The Indians drew back suspiciously and let them go through. It was a tense moment, for it only needed some hothead to hurl a lance and the whole expedition was in jeopardy. And the way those war-painted Indians looked at the blue-uniformed soldiers on their territory, it was plain that many were near-bent on suicide.

But those chiefs played their part well, now. They stood their mounts outside the moving lines of cavalry and faced their people, and it would have been death by their hand if any Cheyenne or Shoshone had raised his lance or drawn a bow-string.

Then the danger moment was passed. The double line of cavalry trotted through, and the Indians came flocking in a close-riding, jostling mass at their rear.

Cheyenne was up with the major now, directing the movements of the troops. As they came out on to the slope opposite the canyon mouth, they could see the battle that was raging at the entrance to it. The Volunteers were lying up in strategic places within a hundred yards of the canyon, their rifles pouring a deadly hail of lead in at the harassed defenders beyond. Other Volunteers were scaling the bluffs in order to get in a position above the Indians. Once they were on top of the canyon, they would be able to fire down upon the unprotected Indians, who would be completely at their mercy. And these men were in no mood to show mercy.

The major ordered the Indians behind them to remain where they were, and to keep out of any more fighting. Cheyenne translated the order to a chief, who rode back to announce it to the following Indians. Then the major ordered his men to close up behind him, and go in at a gallop.

Cheyenne rode out on the south flank with the other four Indian chiefs, so that they would be conspicuous to their fellows within the canyon.

The cavalry came thundering across the low ground, aiming to ride between the warring parties. A yellow dust rose as they charged, almost obscuring them; yet they must have seen that these were the United States forces, because no rifle from the Volunteers opened fire on them.

Instead they began to stand up and cheer, thinking that these were reinforcements. The cheers changed to puzzled frowns as the cavalry wheeled in a solid body between them and the canyon - and not an arrow, not a bullet, was fired by the Indians at the soldiers.

Cheyenne started to wheel round towards the major, when they were abreast of the canyon, but a horse suddenly rode in front of him, blocking his way - a sinewy brown hand grasped his bridle rein and halted his horse.

Quickly he looked round. Those four Indian chiefs were close upon him in a threatening circle - and he was still without arms.

'Jo-shay will stay with us,' a chief said softly. 'Even now it is not too late for the white man to show treachery.'

Cheyenne bowed his head, understanding. These chiefs intended him to be a hostage, as surety that the plan he had instigated was honest and no trap to ensnare the Indians. He was content that it should be so. He had confidence in that army major and felt that the soldier's intentions, too, were honourable.

So he spurred his horse away, apart from the mass of wheeling cavalry, until they came to a green basin in the arid, near-desert at the mouth of the canyon, where seeping moisture provided sustenance for a patch of grass and a few tenacious bushes. There he dismounted, and the red men with him. Then they sat, like sentinels before the mouth of the canyon, and watched the drama unfold before them.

The cavalry had strung out across the mouth of the canyon, and as they came upon the riflemen these were driven before them. The main body of Volunteers was behind some low hills to the north of the canyon, and these came riding forward at this unexpected intervention, and even from that distance Cheyenne could hear the shouts of expostulation.

The major went riding up to meet them, and they could see him get involved in a long and angry argument with

the Volunteers - though the anger was all in the manner
and words of the Kansas men.

'He's tellin' 'em to get back out of the territory,'
Cheyenne thought. 'An' their blood's up, an' they won't go
easily.'

The argument went on a long time, and it became
apparent that the Volunteers did not intend to be
deprived of their full victory. The chiefs alongside
Cheyenne became restless, as they saw the Volunteers
mass threateningly and even begin to move forward.

To the red men it didn't seem reasonable that in the
last resort the officer would go so far in his determination
to save the lives of Indians by ordering his men to open
fire on brother whites.

And yet, when the threatening forward movement of
the Volunteers had begun to have the semblance of a
charge, that was just what he did.

He raised his right hand above his head, and clearly
that had been a prearranged signal. He did it, though he
was surrounded by enemies, and must die himself if his
troopers fired a volley. Yet his hand went up unhesitat-
ingly, and every rifle of those two hundred troopers lifted
to blue shoulders and pointed at the advancing irregulars.

It stopped them. It was one thing charging Indians
with a few old muzzle-loading Henrys and bows and
arrows, but quite another to charge at well-armed, well-
disciplined soldiers. They drew rein, hesitated, then
slowly circled back.

The major lifted his hand again, and now the cavalry
rode slowly forward, driving the Volunteers back until
they were half a mile from the mouth of the canyon. And
then, obstinately, the men from Kansas held their ground;
at that point they gathered determination once more and
refused to retreat.

Again Cheyenne watched the major ride up to the officers among the Hundred Day Volunteers and begin to
parley with them.

'He is a man among men.' Cheyenne heard one of the

chiefs utter the highest compliment that an Indian could bestow on any man. Plainly now these Indian chiefs trusted the major, and that was a good thing for when the time came for peace terms to be discussed.

When night fell, the major was still sitting with the Kansas officers, still obstinately insisting on his way. Cheyenne knew what that way was - the Kansas men must get out of the territory immediately, and so pave the way for an armistice discussion with the tribesmen.

So it was that a hostile force of irregular troops sat out on the plain, while a silent, efficient, little army of cavalry barred their way to the canyon. And between the soldiers and the equally silent, watchful Indians all along that canyon mouth, sat Cheyenne and the Indian chiefs, stolidly awaiting the outcome of all this talk. What Cheyenne feared was that the most desperate among the Kansas men might try to outflank the troops in the dark and attempt their vengeance before they were finally cheated out of it.

He said nothing of this to the chiefs, but he knew it was in their thoughts, too.

And he also knew that if an attack, no matter from what quarter, developed, his life would be forfeit. These Indians were still suspicious of treachery, still sure that most of these white then would seize upon the advantage of their position and inflict their hatred upon the trapped and helpless Indians.

Still not quite certain of Cheyenne Joe's good intentions. For with all their lives at stake, they could not afford to take even the slightest chance.

Just on dusk the chiefs conferred together, and then they approached carrying a rope. The old, old Indian spoke: 'There is such treachery in the hearts of all men that we cannot find trust in anyone, not even in you, O Joshay. We ask you to submit to being bound during the night, so that you, at least, will remain among us if the white men go to attack our kind.'

Cheyenne sighed. He was unarmed - now they wished

to render him completely helpless. Then he held out his hands, because he saw there was nothing he could do about it, anyway. If he tried to resist, that would make them all the more determined to overpower him, and they were in sufficient strength to do so.

But he hated it, when it was done, to have to be there among the bushes and know that he was, for the first time in his adult life, completely helpless and at the mercy of any enemy.

And he couldn't forget that within a few hundred yards of him were men who hated him and wished only to kill him. The followers of White Fox, who would hang if he could give evidence of what they had done in Luther country, and White Fox himself, who had been publicly thrashed and humiliated. That was something no proud Indian could ever forgive - or forget.

CHAPTER TEN

AND BLUE FLOWER WAITED!

Camp-fires flickered and grew where the two armies of men faced each other, but none showed in the canyon where a silent people awaited the first signs of their fate. And long into the night went the debate between the Volunteer officers and the infantry major.

By turning his head, Cheyenne could see the glow of those fires. The four chiefs had gone to sit on the lip of the basin, facing out with unceasing vigilance so as to know the moment danger threatened.

The hours of night passed, and for part of the time, in spite of the constricting bonds, Cheyenne slept. His life had made him philosophical – if he could do nothing further to help in bringing peace, then at least he himself could enjoy peace in sleep.

He was awake, though, when the first pale streaks of light showed over the eastern hills, awake and wondering what the day would bring for him - and for these Indians with him and back in the canyon. The talks must have ended in the night, perhaps to be resumed after daybreak.

Those chiefs were still squatting up there above him, and he heard muttering suddenly and felt that they were braced and alert. He tried to struggle into a sitting position, wanting to know what stealthy sound had made them uneasy, but he failed and had to lie back.

Then he saw one of the shadowy figures slide away out of sight, and he knew that their keen ears had detected the approach of enemies. It gave him a panicky feeling, lying there, to be so helpless and to know that deadly enemies were moving in to attack them. For they could not be Indians moving out of the canyon; the chiefs wouldn't now be facing north if that were so.

Then he heard a soft sound behind him. It was close; so close that he knew he must be within arm's length of whoever crept up to him - only his arms weren't free to reach out to defend himself.

He wasn't gagged, though, and his mouth opened to shout a warning. Then a hand fell across his mouth, silencing him.

It wasn't a strong hand, though, and it didn't press hard. And he knew in an instant who it was.

Blue Flower!

She was crouching close to him, her voice a soft whisper, her hair touching his face as she held her lips to his ear. He could feel the warmth of her breath on his cheek-

She was saying: 'White Fox comes to kill you. He and his followers are ready to escape with the dawn, but before they go they intend to silence you!'

His arms were free. She must have cut them with a sharp knife, though he never saw the movement of the blade. He tried to sit up, but the blood was out of his limbs and she had to help him.

'Come,' she whispered. 'Get away from this place.'

'But what about Grey Wolf and Turkey Head, Leaping Fawn and Man-without-an-ear?'

'They will not be hurt by White Fox.' The girl spoke with certainty. 'But they will kill you!'

And Cheyenne knew that the four chiefs would slay

him, too, if they saw him erect and unbound and talking about flight.

He didn't want to leave those chiefs. They would be sure that he was a traitor to them if they found he had gone. But it seemed better to retire a distance away from that hollow and watch events, rather than remain and be killed.

So he drew back with the girl, inching his way out of the hollow without making a sound. By the way the chiefs were alert it seemed as though White Fox and his men were approaching from the north.

The girl held his hand and led the way. She seemed to have marked out a favourable line of retreat. They were following a tunnel that carried winter flood water off the bare land and into the watershed of the Allardyce basin. Now it way dry, and was like sand to their feet.

The light was suddenly growing stronger. Now - almost in a second, it seemed - they could see each other. Blue Flower was in a panic at the brightening light, trying to hurry him on; for they had taken time in creeping out from he green hollow and were still no more than fifty yards from it.

The sky was beginning to yellow, to change to gold, then to orange. Together they stumbled along the twisting waterway, bent double to keep their heads below the skyline.

And so it was that they ran right into the hands of the Strong Heart, White Fox.

They were rounding a bend that was a miniature chasm rent by torrential rains in the earth: and coming the opposite way, stooped like themselves, loped White Fox and a dozen braves.

For a startled moment they stopped and looked at each other. Then Cheyenne heard a moan of horror come to the lips of the maiden, and she flung herself forward into the line of fire.

At that same moment a shot rang out, only it came from their rear. Everyone straightened to look above the waterway. Grey Wolf went racing past on his horse, followed by Leaping Fawn and Man-without-an-ear. There was no sign of Turkey Head. Perhaps the shot had found its mark in that brave chieftain.

The next moments were confusion and chaos. Cheyenne took advantage of the disturbance to drag the girl back and pull her out of sight round the bend. He heard a shout from White Fox, and then the Indians were after them.

But racing across from the direction of the hollow were white men with rifles held at the ready—

White men. Pengelly. Galbray. And men who might have been the perpetrators of the massacre along Sycamore Creek.

Coming after the fleeing chiefs – and yet they were lost, as if something had happened to surprise them and they weren't sure what next to do. As if, thought Cheyenne, they'd expected to find someone in that hollow, only now he wasn't there, and they hadn't had time to think around the situation.

They never did get a chance. White Fox saw them. White Fox wanted to kill Cheyenne Joe Shay more than anything else in the world - except one thing. That one thing was to keep White Fox alive. So when he saw those advancing white men, he shrilled a warning to his followers and turned to race back to where their horses were picketed.

Cheyenne dragged Blue Flower under an overhang of earth and watched. He saw heavy forms leap down into the watercourse, Pengelly and Galbray among them. Pengelly, Galbray, and those Sycamore Creek killers - they must have sallied out with the same idea as the Indians. They wanted to silence the one man who could give evidence against them, and they didn't care if their efforts were misconstrued by the waiting Indians in the canyon, if it started hostilities all over again.

It was ironical that now those bodies of men, red and white, both wanting to silence the same man, should meet and attack each other and leave the way for their victim to escape. Cheyenne thought: 'If only they knew!'

Some of the white men must have raced ahead of the Indians, perhaps thinking that Cheyenne was among them, and they had trapped White Fox and his followers like rats in a drain. Like cornered rats, then, White Fox and his men came fighting back at their pursuers. They were in greater numbers, too, and were so desperate that the better-armed white men found all in a moment that they had bitten off more than they could chew.

Cheyenne pulled the girl into a retreat along the watercourse. They were unarmed, save for the knife the girl carried, and it was wiser for both to put as much distance as they could between them and the shouting, savagely fighting men.

Once Cheyenne lifted his head above the level of the watercourse, and he saw white man and red locked in murderous embrace; saw rifle-butts striking with brutal force on to shaven heads, and knives lifting and stabbing and tomahawks whirling and descending. Men shrieked with pain, then groaned as they died - but mostly they were the white men who were dying, Cheyenne noticed. Pengelly hadn't expected to meet up with more than a few Indians.

The girl was trembling. He put his arm round her soft body to console her, and helped her along. She had been brought up to a life of constant danger, where death was all too common a phenomenon, and by all the reasoning of Easterners she was therefore a brutalized savage.

But she wasn't, Cheyenne realized now. She was a girl like any other girl, shrinking from the horror of the violence behind her, wanting only to keep her eyes from it and run as far as she could from it all.

Cheyenne tried to console her, as they stumbled along. He panted: 'They are bad men, Blue Flower. They are the men who made this war. It is right and fitting that now they mete out justice one to the other.'

They were running now towards the Indians in the

canyon, still under cover of that waterway. Cheyenne looked up again, northwards this time, and saw the blue-coated cavalry spurring out to hold back a mob of Volunteers, excited by the fighting almost in the mouth of the canyon. At any moment the mob might get out of hand and come racing towards the canyon mouth. Cheyenne paused for breath and looked that way, too.

The Indians were massing, ready to resume the fight. To them it must have looked like another of the white man's tricks, and this time they were finished with the white man and were intent only on sallying out to die bravely on the battlefield.

He had come so near to saving the peace, only to find his efforts all thwarted by Pengelly and his wretched followers. Now there seemed no way of preventing a resumption of hostilities.

Blue Flower screamed. Cheyenne heard her voice rise in utter anguish, so that it came clear to him even above the din of shouting, fighting men fifty yards away.

He whipped round. Pengelly was four or five yards away.

Pengelly had a gun in his hand, but must have known it was empty, for he made no attempt to fire it. Instead he came forward, that heavy gun held aloft to strike him down.

Cheyenne lurched away from the crumbling bank of the watercourse, and as he came he shouted: 'The canyon, Blue Flower. Run to your people!'

He saw her out of the corner of his eye go scrambling up to the higher ground just as he closed with Pengelly. Saw something fall from her hand. That was one good thing - Blue Flower was safely out of this. Now he could defend himself with an easier mind.

Defend—? When he saw that smooth, red-faced man before him, his rage burned away all thoughts of defence and caution. This was the man responsible for a lot of death and suffering - a man completely conscienceless and selfish. Even now he had deserted his followers and left them to fight against the overwhelming odds of the Indians.

The two men clashed. At once Cheyenne got the feeling of mighty strength in those massive limbs. He gripped and tried to throw Pengelly, but the commissioner only snarled and threw back and Cheyenne was near to losing his footing.

Then Pengelly got his hand loose and began to beat him about the head with the gun. Cheyenne kept ducking and so avoided the main force of that descending weapon, and then he gripped the arm again and wrestled the gun out of Pengelly's hand.

When the gun fell free the men parted, panting there at the bottom of that watercourse, crouched and glaring like a pair of wild animals. Then Pengelly came in for the kill. His mighty fists hammered through the ex-Indian agent's defences, smashing into his face so that he was blinded by tears and the blood ran freely into his eyes and mouth.

They rolled to the ground, snarling, gasping, straining, each seeking a death-hold on the other. Pengelly got a grip around Cheyenne's throat, but then lost it because of an almost superhuman effort on the part of his adversary. They mauled again for a few seconds, Pengelly doing every brutal thing to his opponent that he could think of.

And then he gripped Cheyenne's arm, the one that had been stabbed by Blue Flower. A weakened muscle seemed to snap under the paralysing grip of that immensely strong man. Triumph blazed from Pengelly's eyes as the arm became like a useless stick in his hand. Now he would win; now he could kill his hated enemy and then flee to safety.

Pengelly was so sure that he fought himself out of Cheyenne's grip and stood back to reload his gun. He did it calmly, for all the heaving of his chest and the sweat that poured from his red face. And Cheyenne could only lie against the bank and wait until that gun was reloaded and fired at him—

His hand rested on something cold. It was a knife. Blue Flower must have thrown it to him when she fled. It was his only chance to save his life. He hated to do it; hated it the more because Pengelly was over-confident and was slipping the last round into place without even looking at him.

Desperately, Cheyenne threw it. Mexican fashion. Gripping the point of the blade and flicking it with a twist of his wrist towards Pengelly.

Pengelly fired. The bullet struck splinters off a rock and some peppered into Cheyenne's neck, but it did no worse than that. And then Pengelly was sagging forward, holding his throat, falling - dying.

Wearily Cheyenne dragged himself up to the lip of the watercourse. He was in time to see half a dozen braves go riding away east of him. They must be the victors of the fight against Galbray and the others, he thought. Painfully he clambered back along the waterway. He found many dead. Galbray and White Fox were among them, and some who could have been those Sycamore Creek murderers. It seemed that most of his enemies were dead now.

Yet as he stood erect and looked out across the plain, it seemed that the damage they had done might be beyond repair. The troopers were holding back the Volunteers, but reckless mob of Indians, inflamed by what seemed to them to be yet further instances of the white man's treachery, were massing on their ponies, their war bonnets on their heads again, their faces freshly painted.

And Cheyenne saw that many had put on black war-paint - black, the sign of death. These Indians knew it was suicidal, yet they were preparing to go out and fight and kill as many white men as possible before they, too, were killed. It was not in their nature to lie holed up in a canyon and be butchered one by one. If they were to die, they would die on an open battlefield.

Cheyenne had lived with them so long that he understood all this simply by looking at them; he knew the thought in their minds, the way they reasoned things. They would charge any minute now and attack both Volunteers and the hated blue-uniformed American soldiery.

Desperately he clawed his way out into the open. He was a wreck of a man, stumbling over the open ground towards the entrance to that canyon; his clothes were torn and his face and chest were a mass of blood. He felt weak, scarcely able to see and to stand. And yet he willed himself to go forward, to stagger on to where they awaited him. Curiously, strength seemed to return with purpose, so that those last strides were made erect and he looked much like the old Cheyenne Jo-shay those Indians knew.

He stood before them, arms lifted to stay their rush. And he shouted: 'I have come back to you. I am still hostage to the white man's intentions.'

Grey Wolf, that old, old warrior chief, came spurring out. 'More of our people have died,' he shouted. 'Always where you are, Jo-shay, so there is death!' And that old arm lifted to throw his lance.

Cheyenne Joe stood, not trying to avoid the blow, not even caring if it did come. It seemed that he had lost.

And then the lance came slowly down. He heard Grey Wolf's mumbling voice: 'I love this man as a son. I cannot do it.' And he rode away.

Cheyenne lifted up his voice again. 'Why do you not hold your weapons until we have held a pow-wow together? You can kill me then as easily as you can kill me now. All I ask is that you hear my voice, so that I can tell you there was no treachery during the night.

'There were men who wanted to kill me, both white men and Indians, but they slew only themselves. See, the soldiers hold back the white men who would continue with this war. The good major is keeping his word, and he will keep it while you hold the peace. But the moment you attack him, he will have to turn on you and join with the other white men in the fighting against you.'

His words were finding listeners. On the fringe of the

crowd Cheyenne could see the stooped head of wise old Grey Wolf and knew that the old man was listening. So he lifted his voice and spoke to him.

'You are honoured above all in the Cheyenne Nation for the wisdom that goes with your grey hairs, O Grey Wolf. Let your people hear your voice counselling peace for a further hour until it becomes apparent what the intentions of the white man are. See, I will stay with you. I put myself at your mercy, and if the white man attacks, then my life shall be yours.'

At once angry voices shouted against the idea, and lances were raised to crash against war shields. Many were there who would not believe that the soldiers had for once come to the defence of their recent enemies, and they shouted to take Jo-shay's scalp and then thunder on for a final great battle with the white oppressors.

But Grey Wolf showed himself a leader of men just then, a man who could continue the tradition of that other great Cheyenne chief, Black Bear. He rode before them and lifted his hand for silence.

'It was in my heart to kill Jo-shay for the traitor he seemed to be.' His wrinkled, mahogany face turned to look again at their former agent, as if to satisfy his old eyes that what he had once seen was still there. And he seemed satisfied. 'But I saw only honesty in this man. When I made to kill him he did not try to defend himself, and on his face was neither fear nor anger. Instead he looked like a man with sorrow in his heart for the things that were proposed against him.'

Grey Wolf raised his voice. 'Such a man should not die. Such a man is truly our friend, and with a friend like him we might still find peace for our squaws and papooses. Do you not see, you men who are blind with the passion of war, if a man is as honest as Jo-shay seems to be - as I swear Jo-shay is - then his words must be heeded. If he offers even one chance in a thousand of escape for our people, then we must take it. For I see no escape for anyone if we go riding out now to make war again with the white man.'

The Indian throng stirred and muttered to each other, and yet still the loudest voices were raised in anger against the proposition.

Cheyenne called again, 'Just one hour - that's all I ask.' And then he went to a bare rock back in the entrance, close to where the women and children were thronging, and he sat down with his aching head in his hands.

After a while he looked up. Some of the Indians were dismounting. His heart jumped. He might yet win. And then his heart beat again, frantically, madly. For Blue Flower, slim and graceful, was coming towards him with a wooden bowl of water in her hands.

But panic came immediately upon the elation. He called, 'Go back, Blue Flower. If things go hard with me they will not forget my friends. Remember what happened to Black Bear.'

She came on without pause, however, her eyes modestly on the ground before her. So he said, weakly, because he could think of nothing else to say just then, 'And you hate all white men, remember?'

She lifted her eyes at that. There was no hatred in them for anyone. Cheyenne sighed and relaxed, and somehow was satisfied. Before the eyes of her people, Blue Flower bathed his wounds and bandaged them. Then she went and sat at his feet, and Cheyenne knew what that meant.

Blue Flower had chosen him as her man. She had tied her fortunes with his. If I die, he found himself thinking - and then he checked the thought as a stir of sound floated in to him from the massed Indians below.

He looked to see what had caused the interest, and he saw a sight that brought him to his feet.

'Blue Flower,' he called. 'They go - see, they go!'

For the Volunteers were mounting and riding disconsolately eastwards, and close behind them as if still not trusting them, rode the vigilant soldiers.

Then the tension broke among the Indians. Women came running down to their men, thankful that they would not have to ride out to their death. Children came and were held up to others who had thought never to see them again. And then everyone went slowly into the canyon to a great council around a ceremonial fire.

Cheyenne was first to stand and speak. 'You have seen that there are men among the white race who can behave honourably. I say go, right now, and meet with that gallant soldier at Allardyce Springs and make peace with him.'

'And you, O Jo-shay?' someone called - perhaps someone who still had a shred of suspicion.

'I,' said Joe Shay, 'will stay on in the reservation. I will live with you, I will be even as a Cheyenne while you are at peace.'

He turned. Lovely Blue Flower was standing with the womenfolk, but she could hear. He looked into those brown, melting eyes, and he called, 'I will take a wife among the Cheyennes if there is any woman who will have me.'

Blue Flower came forward at that - one step, and then she halted, a flush of shame on her face that she had been seen to respond so eagerly to the white man's call.

So Cheyenne strode across to her, where she stood trembling and uncertain. He put his arm round her and said, 'Blue Flower has said she will be my wife. So it is now I am one of you.'

There was triumph in his soul that he had never thought to experience. He had defeated his enemies, he had achieved the peace between white men and red that he desired, and lovely Blue Flower was to be his bride. What more could a man want?

And then Grey Wolf paid him final a honour.

'I am satisfied, O people of the Cheyennes. There is no evil in the heart of Jo-shay towards us. I say, then, let Jo-shay go and make the best peace terms for us at Allardyce Springs. Such a voice will speak well for the red man.'

And so it was. It was Cheyenne Joe Shay who went in the end with Grey Wolf and other chiefs to meet the gallant major, Joe Shay who secured favourable terms, including a continuation of the bounty payments for the Cheyennes. And when that was done, when all were satisfied, he rode back with the chieftains to their camp in the hills.

And Blue Flower was waiting for him.